Egghead

AN ALDO ZELNICK COMIC NOVEL

Written by Karla Oceanak

Illustrated by Kendra Spanjer

BAILIWICK PRESS

This is a work of fiction. Names, characters, places, and incidents are either the product of the author's imagination or are used fictitiously. Any resemblance to actual persons, living or dead, events, or locales is entirely coincidental.

First trade paperback edition 2016

Published by:
Bailiwick Press
309 East Mulberry Street
Fort Collins, Colorado 80524
(970) 672-4878
Fax: (970) 672-4731
www.bailiwickpress.com
www.aldozelnick.com

Book design by:
Launie Parry
Red Letter Creative
www.red-letter-creative.com

ISBN 978-1-934649-69-5

Library of Congress Control Number: 2016931916

Dear Aldo –

You exceed* my expectations* each and every day.

Everlastingly* yours,

Goosy

ARNALDO,

¡Siempre llueve sobre mojado!

Señor Mot

WHO'S WHO

ME – ALDO ZELNICK.

MI MEJOR AMIGO, JACK.

ALBERT EINSTEIN. SCIENTIST. COOL DUDE.

ABUELO AND MRS. LOPEZ.

SEÑOR ESPINOZA, MY EVIL ESPAÑOL* TEACHER.

MR. MOT, MY ERUDITE* NEIGHBOR.

TOMMY GELLER, FRIENDSNATCHER.

MY OTHER FRIENDS, DANNY AND BEE.

BACON BOY, MY COMIC CHARACTER.

MY GRANDMA, GOOSY. GUTSY LADY.

MY MOM & DAD.

MY DOG, MAX, AND JACK'S DOG, SLATE.

MY OLDER BROTHER, TIMOTHY.

5

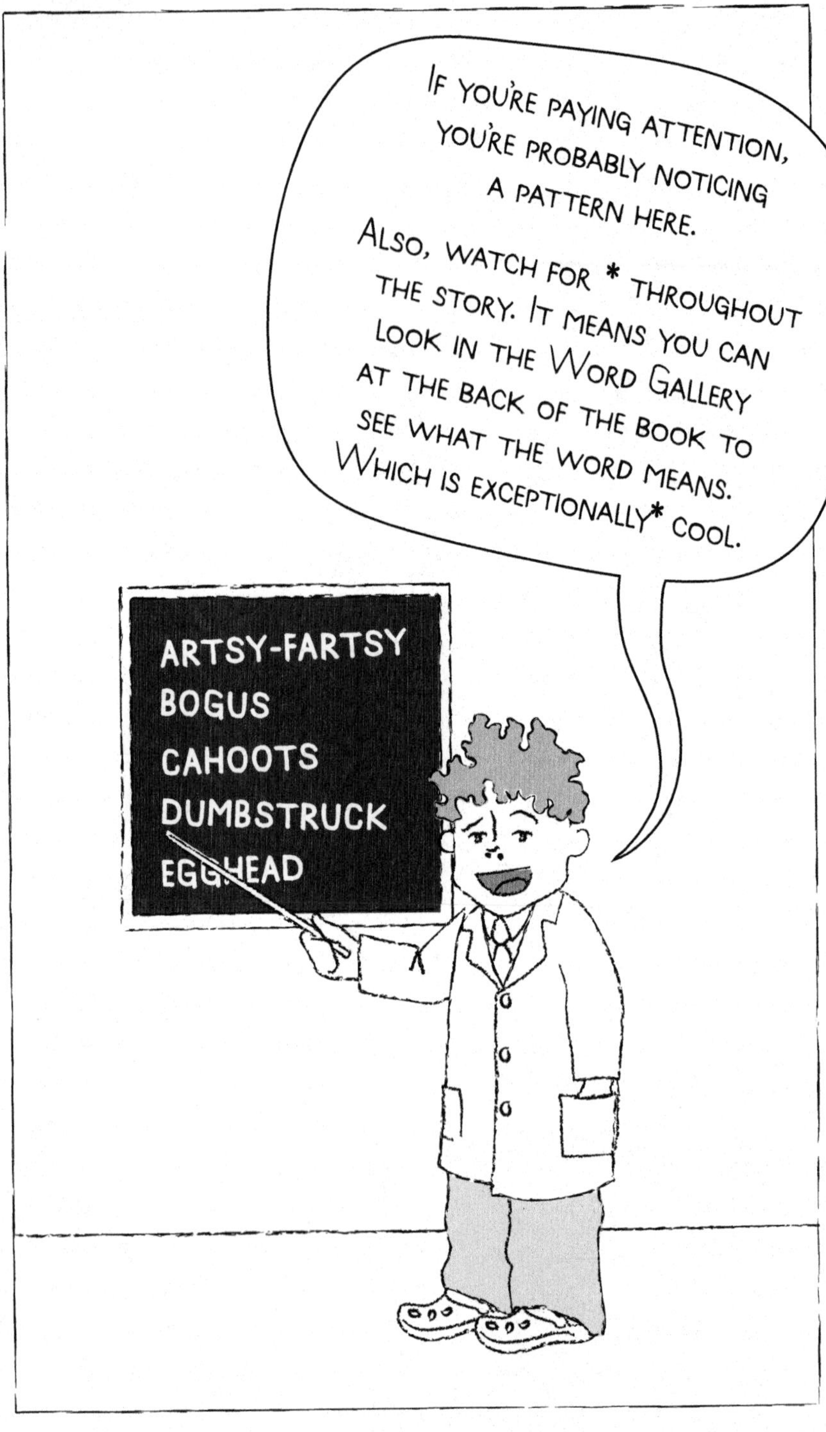
IF YOU'RE PAYING ATTENTION, YOU'RE PROBABLY NOTICING A PATTERN HERE.
ALSO, WATCH FOR * THROUGHOUT THE STORY. IT MEANS YOU CAN LOOK IN THE WORD GALLERY AT THE BACK OF THE BOOK TO SEE WHAT THE WORD MEANS. WHICH IS EXCEPTIONALLY* COOL.
ARTSY-FARTSY
BOGUS
CAHOOTS
DUMBSTRUCK
EGGHEAD

ROLL OF THUNDER

It's a dark and stormy night all right.

I was in my bed, minding my own business, when an earsplitting* kaboom! of thunder catapulted me halfway across the room. Seriously, one second I was dead asleep...

and the next I was on the floor, rolled up in my covers like a human burrito!

As I lay there burritofied, lightning flickered and thunder growled. I could hear the splatting rain and the moaning wind and the clacking tree branches as they extended* their long, twisted claws to tap at my window. Max was trembling at my feet.

Good thing it's not almost Halloween or this would be super eerie,* I thought.

AHHHHHHH! TRAPPED IN MY OWN SECURITY BLANKET!

AND YOU THOUGHT THAT OTHER KID WAS WIMPY...

DO I LOOK SCARED TO YOU?

Wait a second! I remembered. It's October! Halloween is just 18 days away! So I speedily unrolled myself and grabbed Max, to calm him down.

Lightning flashed again, and I tiptoed over to my window to look outside. Pitch blackness and soaking-wet raininess. Another pop of lightning... and I saw him. A mysterious figure with a black umbrella. He was standing in the middle of the street, and he was looking up at me!

I ducked down and hyperventilated for a couple seconds. When I peeked back over the windowsill, the street was empty.

Whoa. That was creeeepy. Who <u>was</u> that person, and what was he doing outside in the middle of the night in the middle of a thunderstorm?

Welp, I can't fall back asleep now, so I might as well read a chapter or two. My school library lady hooked me up with the comic book version of *A Wrinkle in Time*, which is an old story about these kids with scientist parents. The kids get woken up in the middle of the night by a thunderstorm (Hey! Just like me!) and decide to eat liverwurst-and-cream-cheese sandwiches.

Hm. I don't know what liverwurst is, but I just realized I'm so hungry I could eat a horse. Plus, food has a way of calming me. And downstairs, in the kitchen, there's a fresh batch of chocolate éclairs* Dad made that are calling my name...

ALDO!
OH, ALLLDDDOOO!

RAINDROPS KEEP FALLIN' ON MY HEAD

What mother would make her kid walk to school in a downpour? I'll give you one guess.

"But it's raining!" I argued.

"That's what umbrellas are for," she pointed out helpfully.

So I took an umbrella and grumbled my way down to Jack's house. He was waiting for me at the street corner, next to the bent stop sign.

MRS. ENCK RAN INTO IT WITH HER EL CAMINO LAST WEEK. SHEESH. OLD PEOPLE SHOULD PAY MORE ATTENTION!

11

"¿Qué onda?" yelled Jack, who has annoyingly been trying to teach me Spanish ever since he got assigned to be my partner in Spanish class.

Jack is bilingual. His mom's family is from Mexico, and they speak Spanish and English together in a word casserole that makes me a little queasy. Why is Spanish so impossible to comprehend?!

"Uh...it's raining," I said, guessing at what Jack was trying to say. "And I'm exhausted* because that thunder demolished my sleep last night."

"I know!" said Jack. "It woke up everyone in my house too—even my abuelo."

Abuelo. What did that mean again? Tree? "The thunder woke up your tree?" I was close enough to Jack by now that I could see him roll his eyes.

"Abuelo means grandpa, doofus," he said. "He just got here from Mexico yesterday. He's staying with my mom and me for a while."

C'MON THUNDER... WHY CAN'T YOU JUST "LEAF" ME ALONE?!

"Ooh, does that mean your mom will make *empanadas?**" Mrs. Lopez cooks all sorts of delectable stuff whenever her big family gets together.

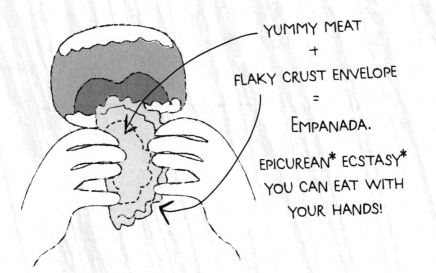

YUMMY MEAT
+
FLAKY CRUST ENVELOPE
=
EMPANADA.

EPICUREAN* ECSTASY* YOU CAN EAT WITH YOUR HANDS!

"Yuck. Probably," groaned Jack, who barely eats anything. Have you noticed how skinny that kid is? His ankles are the size of my pinkie. Jack doesn't even like to talk about food, not even delicious meat pies, so he changed the subject by asking, "What are you gonna be for Halloween?"

"I dunno. Reaper." The Grim Reaper is obviously the greatest costume ever because all you need is a black robe with a hood. Pick up a plastic axe dealie and boom, you're the Reaper. Jack, he's usually a skeleton. Not a big stretch.

HOW MANY TIMES DO I HAVE TO TELL YOU? IT'S NOT PLASTIC. AND IT'S NOT CALLED AN AXE!

"We should be something cool this year," he said.

"Like?"

"Like...elves or dwarves or something." Jack's been all about fantasy ever since he started playing Dungeons & Dragons with Tommy Geller last summer. "Plus, I don't think my skeleton costume fits me anymore."

"Hey!" I just remembered. "Speaking of skeletons, I saw some creepy person standing in the street during the storm last night! I mean, who's crazy enough to go out in the pouring rain unless they're forced to by their mothers?"

Just then, a blob of shocking pink whizzed by.
"Hello, Aldoooooooo!" it called.

It was my grandma, Goosy. She's for sure crazy enough to go out in a rainstorm even when she doesn't have to.

WHAT AM I GONNA BE?

After dinner, Mom was looking at old Halloween pictures on her laptop. Man, when you're little, your parents sure can get a lot of mileage out of one tiny piece of candy. Apparently I'd wear anything if they just gave me a Dum-Dum.

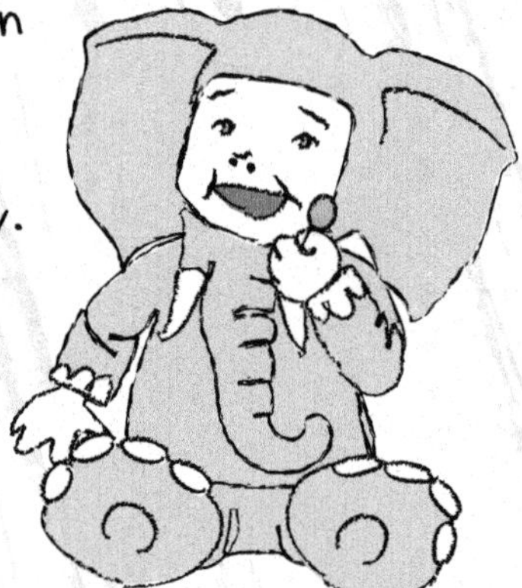

AGE ZERO

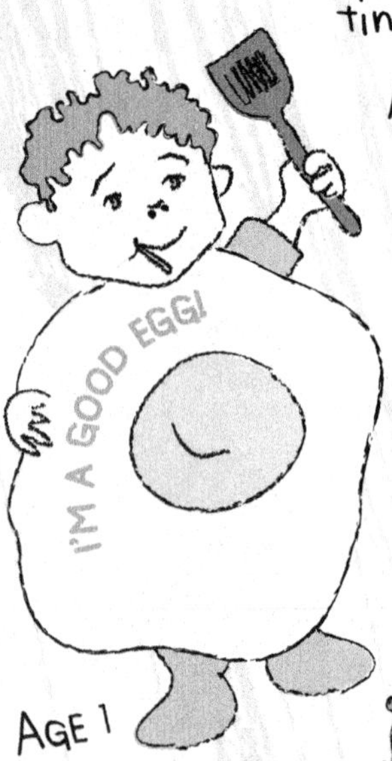
I'M A GOOD EGG!

AGE 1

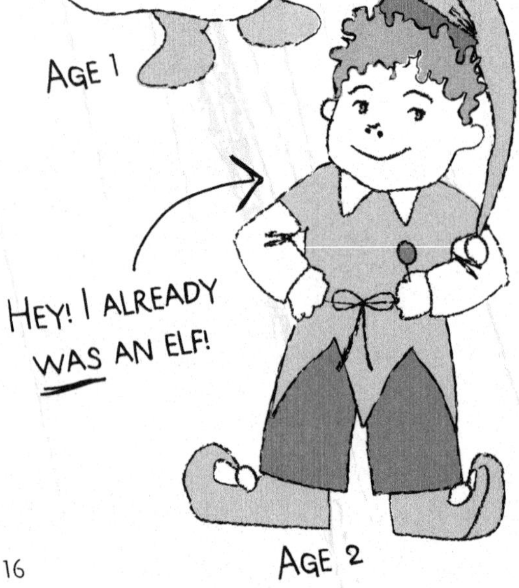
HEY! I ALREADY WAS AN ELF!

AGE 2

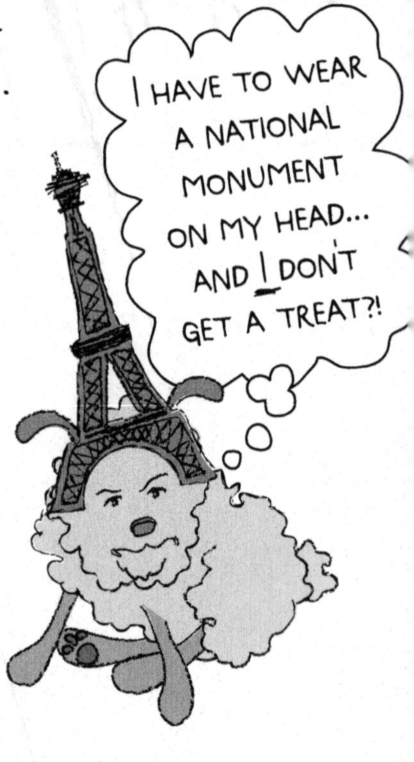
I HAVE TO WEAR A NATIONAL MONUMENT ON MY HEAD... AND I DON'T GET A TREAT?!

But maybe Jack's right. Maybe we should come up with better costumes this year. After all, Halloween is my second-favorite holiday. And it would be cool to be a zombie or a sumo wrestler or a ninja chef or something.

When I asked my brother, Timothy, what he was going to be for Halloween, he said high schoolers are too old to trick-or-treat.

"Pfffft," I said. "I'm getting a sackful of free candy every October 31st until I'm ancient. They'll have to pry the bag from my cold, dead hands."

"Charming, bro."

AS SOON AS I WAS OLD ENOUGH TO KNOW BETTER, I STARTED USING A PILLOWCASE FOR TRICK-OR-TREATING INSTEAD OF THAT DIMINUTIVE PUMPKIN BUCKET THEY TRICKED ME INTO USING WHEN I WAS LITTLE.

THAT'S RIGHT. HIT THE ROAD, JACK.

BOO-HOO

Hey, instead of a ninja, maybe I could be a luchador wrestler like in that movie I saw on TV last weekend called *Nacho Libre!*

Hm. Not sure if shirtless is my best look.

Or whoa, I could be a plate of nachos!

Note to self: Invent edible* costumes.

WRINKLE ME THIS

It's storming again, and the thunder's so loud it keeps vibrating my bed. I think it's even bothering Bogus, my betta fish, because he's got a "what the heck?" look on his face. It never rains this much in Colorado! Sheesh. It better not rain on Halloween...because all my lovely candy will get soggy.

This *Wrinkle in Time* book is kinda bizarre. After the kids eat their sandwiches in the middle of the dark and stormy night, an old homeless lady called Mrs. Whatsit comes to their house and takes them outside to meet her eccentric* old lady friends, Mrs. Who and Mrs. Which.

> YES, I CAN HEAR! MY EARS ARE INSIDE MY BODY, NOT ALL STICKING OUT LIKE YOURS, ALDO.

Then the 3 W ladies evaporate* the kids through a wormhole—which is a wrinkle in time and space—to a faraway planet where the kids' dad is a prisoner. He's an important physics scientist who does top-secret work for the United States government, and he's been captured by an evil alien ruler. The old ladies tell the kids they can save their dad, even though it will be <u>extremely</u> dangerous and scary. (Oh, and the ladies can't help; the kids have to do it all by themselves. Of course. Kids always have to do everything.)

The thunder outside and the scariness inside reminded me of the person with the black umbrella.

So I just crawled over to my window and peeked out, but no one was there. Whew.

IF ALL RULERS WERE GOOD, WHO WOULD WEAR THESE TINY BLACK MOUSTACHES AND EPAULETS?*

A DIFFERENT KIND OF EVIL RULER

Hm. I wonder if _I_ would be courageous enough to risk my life in order to save someone, like the kids in the book do. And I wonder if scientists really will discover how to travel through time and space instantly. If I could wrinkle my way somewhere right this second, I'd go to...

Ack. Mom just marched into my room and told me I have to play my trumpet or else. I asked or else what? She said or else you'll have to find out what the or else is, which from the tone of her voice didn't sound like the best option. Band sure would be a lot more fun if you didn't have to practice.

To THE TUNE OF "RAIN, RAIN, GO AWAY...":

MOM, MOM, GO AWAY,
COME AGAIN ANOTHER DAY.
ALDO WANTS TO DISOBEY.
MOM, MOM, GO AWAY.

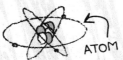
ATOM

ALL CHARGED UP

Today in science we talked about atoms, which was boring because we already learned about them in 4th grade!

Have you ever noticed that school is like that? They like to teach you the same things over and over again...blah, blah, blah.

Good thing EcoWeek is coming up soon. At least that won't be boring. It's a school trip to the mountains just for us 5th graders, because we'll be moving on to middle school next year. I guess it's a way for our teachers to get used to the idea of missing us.

ELECTRON

Anyway, back to atoms. You know, they're those too-tiny-to-see bits

PROTON
NEUTRON

that everything in the universe is supposedly made of. And atoms themselves are made of tinier bits called neutrons and protons, which live in the nucleus in the middle of the atom, and even teensier pieces called electrons* that whiz in circles around the nucleus.

But Mr. Krug didn't just <u>talk</u> about atoms or draw them for us on the Smart Board. Oh no... He took us down to the gym and made us pretend to be a <u>human</u> oxygen atom!

JACK GOT TO JUST CHILLAX IN THE NUCLEUS, BUT MR. KRUG MADE <u>ME</u> A WHIZZING ELECTRON—IN THE OUTER CIRCLE. HELLO! THIS IS SCIENCE CLASS, NOT P.E.!

AND IF I'M PART OF AN <u>OXYGEN</u> ATOM, HOW COME I'M SO OUT OF BREATH, FOR PETE'S SAKE?!

On the way back to our classroom, Jack was whispering to me about his *abuelo*, but I was still mouth-breathing from all that running, so I didn't really catch what he was saying...something about atoms and top-secret laboratories.

But I didn't get a chance to ask him because as soon as we got back to our room, Mr. Krug got busy assigning us a project. Groan. "Project" is just sneaky teacher-language for extra homework.

He gave us a list of famous scientists and said we have to write a report about one of them. Albert Einstein's on the list. I guess he could be <u>kinda</u> interesting. We have a couple things in common, anyway:

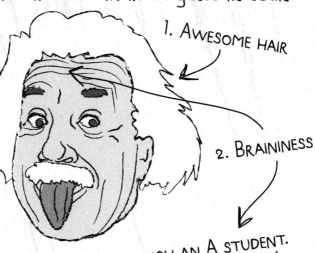

1. AWESOME HAIR

2. BRAININESS

YEAH, I'M PRETTY MUCH AN A STUDENT.
(AS IF YOU COULDN'T HAVE GUESSED...)

LIBRARY TIME

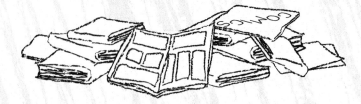

Lunch is my favorite subject, but Library isn't half-bad either. The library at my school has copious cool books (like the *Wrinkle in Time* comic book), a nice librarian, and, best of all, 3 cushy chairs.

Have you ever noticed that when you're a kid, you don't get a padded desk chair like your teacher does? Oh no. <u>You</u> have to sit on rock-hard plastic 7 hours a day. But once a week, if you're fast enough to nab one of the 3 good chairs at Dana Elementary's library, you can relax into cushiony softness for 15 minutes. Ahhh...

MISS TURNER, MY LIBRARY TEACHER (SHE'S ONE OF THOSE GROWN-UPS WITH BRACES.)

So whenever we have Library, I usually grab a Calvin and Hobbes and speed-walk to good-chair central. Today, though, we had to check out a book about a scientist for our reports. Miss Turner had spread out all the science biographies on a table for us to look over. There were books on people named Ernest Just and Percy Lavon and Carl Linnaeus and a couple others no one had ever heard of. Two or three books on Galileo were in the mix...and so were a few about Einstein.

Q. WHAT DO PLANETS READ?

A. COMET BOOKS!

Everybody reached for the Einsteins. He was obviously the only Kit Kat in a pillowcaseful of Tootsie Rolls. Somehow (it might have involved elbowing* Marvin Shoemaker aside) I managed not only to snag a book with Einstein's picture on the cover but also to get the last comfy chair! Yesss! I sank down to enjoy my victory and start reading up on crazy old Albert.

But I couldn't read it! It was a picture book, the kind for little kids with lots of photos and drawings mixed in with the writing. But the letters were some weird combination I couldn't understand. I was just starting to feel totally discombobulated when Jack plopped down on the floor next to me.

THIS IS THE MOST BEWILDERING BOOK I'VE EVER SEEN.

"¿Quién fue Albert Einstein?" said Jack.

"What?"

"That's the title of the book you're reading. It means 'Who was Albert Einstein?' Good job working on your Spanish, Aldo!"

"Arg! <u>That's</u> why I couldn't read it." I needed to go exchange* the book, but I didn't want to give up my chair, so I just slumped there, glaring at Jack. "I don't want a book in dumb Spanish. Why are there Spanish books in our school anyway!"

"Because in case you haven't noticed, some kids at our school speak Spanish." Jack was kinda glaring back at me. "Actually, a lot of kids do. Like me."

"Yeah, but English is your <u>real</u> language."

Jack's face and voice got quieter then. "They're both real," he sighed. "If you want, I'll read the book for you and tell you what it says, in English."

"Nah. I'll get a different one," I said.

But of course, by the time I made it back to the science book table, all the Einsteins had disappeared.

A QUESTION THAT JUST OCCURRED TO ME:

IF THERE'S A WRINKLE IN TIME, WHY DON'T YOU JUST IRON IT?

A IS FOR AUDACIOUS

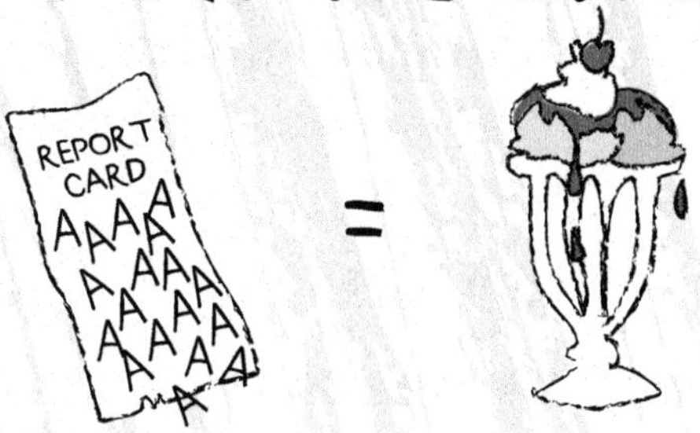
REPORT CARD
=

I brought home my mid-term report card today and presented it to my parents and Goosy at dinner. 6 A's! I figured that was at least worth chocolate pudding for dessert—or maybe something better, like a sundae with whipped cream and those bright-red cherries I'm so enamored* of.

"I'm getting straight A's again," I announced, whipping out the paper with my grades on it. "Not like it's a big deal or anything."

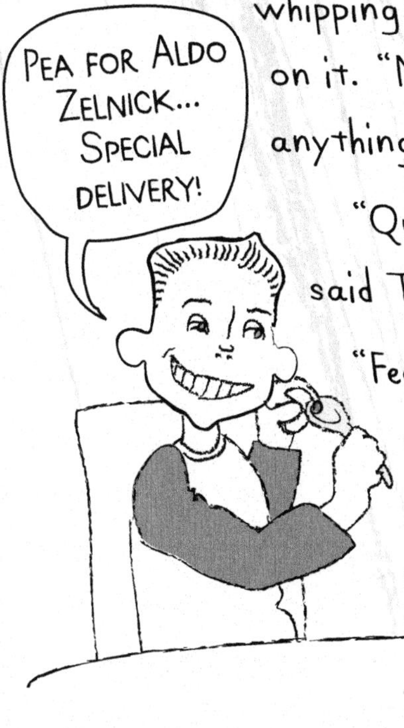
PEA FOR ALDO ZELNICK... SPECIAL DELIVERY!

"Quit being a show-off, Aldo," said Timothy.

"Feel free to share your report card," I told him. Instead, he celebrated my awesomeness by catapulting a pea at me.

"My grandson the egghead!*" exclaimed* Goosy, leaning over to plant a sloppy, wet kiss on my cheek.

"Nice work, sport!" said Dad. "Were you thinking hot fudge sundaes or chocolate malts?"

"Ooh, chocol...," I started to say, but Mom, who had put on her reading glasses to examine the report card, cut me off.

"Egads,* you're getting a D in Spanish, Aldo," she said, the beginnings of a conniption rising in her voice.

"Pffft. It's just Spanish. I only have it 2 days a week. It's barely even a class! Plus, it took me years to learn English, which, by the way, I'm getting an A in. Besides, my Spanish teacher is mean!"

JUST SPANISH?!!!

"He's mean?" asked Dad.

"Yeah! He just expects me to understand what he's saying!"

Timothy was dancing on his chair now, holding the report card above his head like it was a winning lottery ticket. "Aldo's getting a Dee-eee," he sing-songed. "Tee-hee-hee-hee-hee."

"Well, a D is unacceptable," said Mom, "in any language. I'll talk to your Spanish teacher tomorrow to see what you need to do to bring up your grade. Meanwhile, no chocolate celebration."

I turned to Dad, but his lips were straight and he was raising one eyebrow at me in a look that meant, "Don't even go there." Goosy, she just said "¡Te amo!" and started clearing the dishes.

So here I am in my room, dessertless. The rain is beating against my windows and the thunder is booming—a cacophony of despair. I'm supposed to be studying my Spanish vocabulary, but who can remember that *almuerzo* means "lunch" and *gordo* means "fat"? They don't sound anything like the things they're supposed to mean!

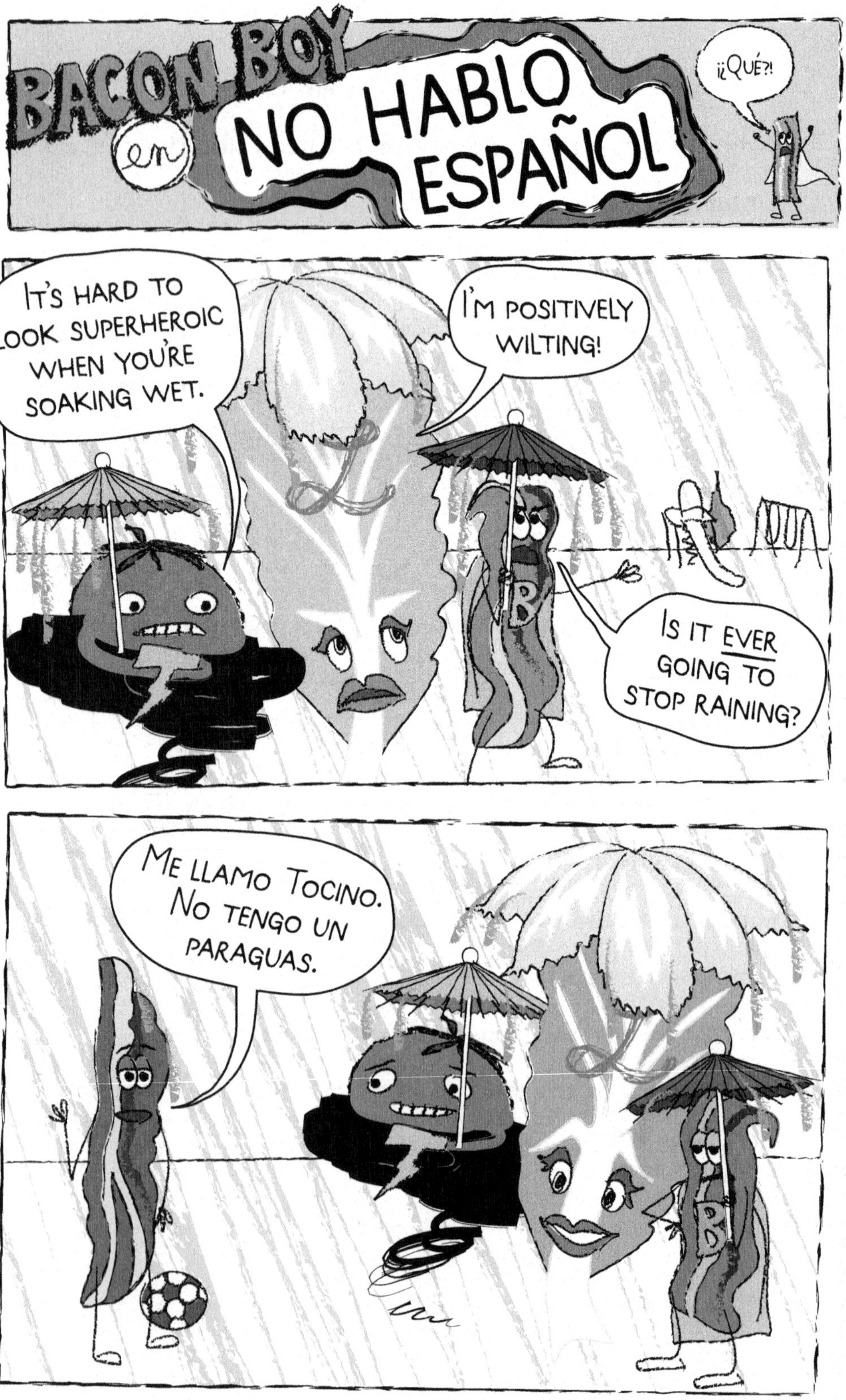
BACON BOY
en
NO HABLO ESPAÑOL
¡¿QUÉ?!
IT'S HARD TO LOOK SUPERHEROIC WHEN YOU'RE SOAKING WET.
I'M POSITIVELY WILTING!
IS IT EVER GOING TO STOP RAINING?
ME LLAMO TOCINO. NO TENGO UN PARAGUAS.

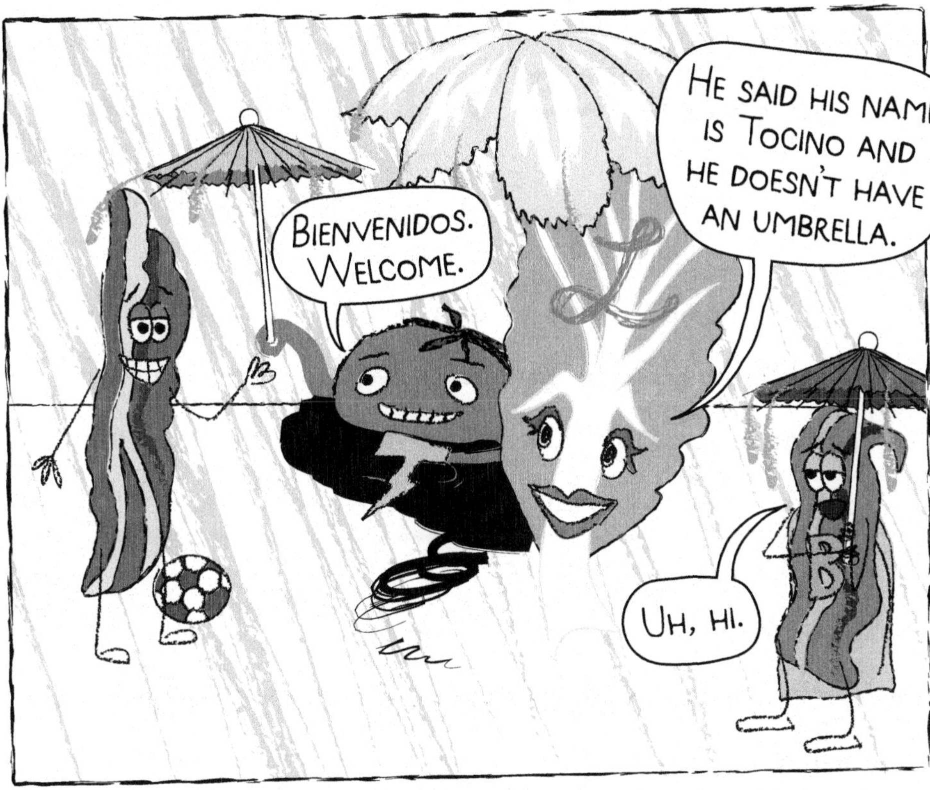
Bienvenidos. Welcome.
He said his name is Tocino and he doesn't have an umbrella.
Uh, hi.

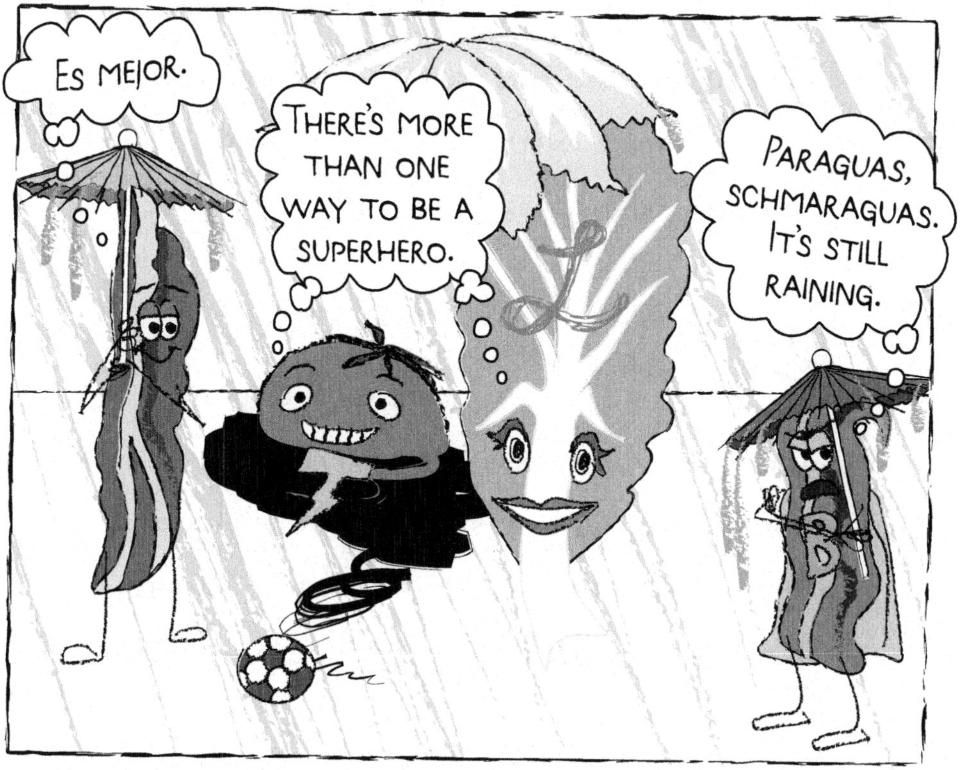
Es mejor.
There's more than one way to be a superhero.
Paraguas, schmaraguas. It's still raining.

SNACKS AT JACK'S

$$E = MC^2$$

(EMPANADAS = MOUTHWATERING CUISINE TIMES 2?)

Remember how I said Mrs. Lopez might make empanadas because her father—Jack's grandpa—is visiting? Good ol' Jack called me after school today to say that she DID make them and there were tons of extras and I should come have one. (Or, I figured, 3 or 4.)

When I walked into Jack's mom-house, it smelled like spicy warmness and sounded like a happy, noisy restaurant—all chatter and laughter and clinking glasses and forks. I followed Jack to the kitchen, where every square inch of the counter was covered with Lopez family delicacies.

I filled a plate with empanadas and other yumminess then moved into the living room, where all Jack's aunts and uncles and cousins were gathered around a little old man with a brown, raisiny face and combed gray hair.

"That's Abuelo," said Jack. "He's 88."

"Holy cow," I said. "He's the oldest human I've ever seen!" I chewed thoughtfully for a moment then pointed a forkful of tamale dripping in sauce at Jack and added, "But if he's gotten to eat food like this for almost a century, he's lived a good life."

"Gross," said Jack. "But yeah, he's pretty amazing. He has 7 sons and daughters and a bunch of us grandkids And he's a scientist. Or at least, he was."

"They have scientists in Mexico?"

"Duh. He even met Einstein once. That's what I was trying to tell you at school."

"He DID? I'm gonna ask him if Einstein's feet stank."

I MANAGED TO GET A FEW BOOKS ON EINSTEIN AT THE PUBLIC LIBRARY. COOL FACTS:

1. HE DIDN'T WEAR SOCKS.

2. HE HARDLY EVER COMBED HIS HAIR.

3. A COMPASS HIS FATHER GAVE HIM WHEN HE WAS 5 WAS HIS FAVORITE TOY.

"Abuelo doesn't talk much anymore," shrugged Jack. "And when he does, it's in Spanish."

"He doesn't speak English?"

"I guess not. He used to."

"Drag."

Later (after I'd learned that empanadas are for dessert, too, because Mrs. Lopez brought me one filled with sweet potatoes and dusted with powdered sugar!), Jack introduced me to Abuelo.

"*Este es mi amigo* Aldo Zelnick," said Jack. "Aldo, this is Señor Egberto Lopez."

AND I THOUGHT MR. MOT WAS ANCIENT.

I smiled my best "I'm-the-amigo-who-doesn't-speak-Spanish" smile and said, "Your name is Egberto?" Ack. I meant to say, "Nice to meet you," but that's not what my ears heard come out of my mouth.

But Abuelo didn't seem to mind. He just smiled back at me with his watery brown eyes then shuffled on down the hallway. I watched him open the door to the coat closet, step inside it, then close the door behind him.

"What kind of scientist was your grandfather, anyway?" I asked Jack.

"He did physics, like Einstein," said Jack. "When he was in college, he got to go on a trip to America and he met Einstein, at a school where Einstein was a professor."

"Sweet! Did he bring him empanadas? I bet Einstein would have liked empanadas."

"I don't know! I remember Abuelo said that one night he was at the college where Einstein taught, and he saw Einstein playing a violin in his office. Plus, he told me that later on, during World War 2, Einstein's equations* were used to figure out how to make an atom bomb. Abuelo even worked for a while as a Level 1 scientist at the super-secret laboratory in New Mexico where the first atom bombs were made."

"Wow. For a mad scientist, Abuelo has really tidy hair."

Jack's grandfather may not talk much, but what if it's because he's still doing secret science? Maybe that's why he's hiding in that closet.

UNLESS YOU'RE A COAT, YOU PROBABLY SHOULDN'T BE HANGING OUT IN CLOSETS. THAT'S THE KIND OF THING THAT MAKES PEOPLE THINK YOU'RE ECCENTRIC.

ANOTHER WRINKLE

I was on the couch reading before bed tonight when Mr. Mot walked into the living room. He and my dad had been in our basement practicing electric guitar.

"Ah, you're reading A Wrinkle In Time," he said. "A science fiction classic with eerie extraterrestrials* and erudite* children who escape their earthly confines. Perfect for this dark and stormy Halloween season."

Mr. Mot just talks like that. You get used to it. "Uh, yeah," I said.

"I am fortunate to own a first edition,*" he added, "signed by its esteemed* author, Madeleine L'Engle."

KNOCK KNOCK.
(WHO'S THERE?)
GUITAR.
(GUITAR WHO?)
GUIT-AR COATS—
IT'S REALLY RAINING OUTSIDE!

"Oh," I said, and I yawned hugely to hint that I would rather read the book in the few minutes I had left before bed than talk about some lady named Madeleine.

"Well, the hour has come for me to depart," Mr. Mot said. "I see it is still precipitating. I am fortunate to have brought my slicker and umbrella." And with that, he put on a raincoat and a hat with a wide brim, tossed his long scarf over his shoulder, and popped open a black umbrella.

"Hey!" I said. "Were you the one I saw out in the storm the other night?!"

"Wild nights are my glory," he said as he stepped out my front door into the rain, "but I..." The wind carried Mr. Mot's final words away as he hurried off into the darkness.

Old people are crazy, I've decided. Goosy, Mr. Mot, Mrs. Enck, Einstein, Abuelo. They do silly things, and they don't care what the rest of us think. They're sort of like toddlers, only with gray hair and drivers' licenses.

LIFE OF
THE PARTY

Today my dad took Jack and me to the costume store downtown. It's the coolest place ever, chock-full of masks, hats, capes, weapons, fake blood—everything you need for Halloween.

Jack found some elf ears and a bow and arrow. I tried on a million things, like a Viking helmet, a penguin mask, and squirrel underpants. (Ha! Just checking to see if you were paying attention. I didn't actually try on any squirrel underpants, but in case the squirrel who lives in your neighborhood needs a fresh pair, they DO sell them at this store.)

I PREFER BOXERS OVER TIGHTY-WHITIES!

Oh, and a bunch of zombies were walking around the store like, well, zombies. Even though it's not Halloween yet, lots of people had on zombie costumes for some reason, including this dreadful-looking lady who walked up to me and asked where I got the great wig I was wearing.

"This isn't a wig. It's my <u>hair</u>."→

"Oh...Well I work here, in the Wig World part of the store...and so I noticed your wig...I mean hair...," she said awkwardly. "Umm...maybe you'd like to try on a wig?"

"Wigs are for girls."

"Pffft. We have loads of boy wigs."

So zombie lady showed me wigs that make you look like Dracula or an Oompa Loompa or Justin Bieber (ew). She climbed on a ladder to get a long, yellow wig for Jack. And that's when I saw it, perched high on the shelf—a wig with wild white hair sticking out in all directions. Einstein! She got it down for me and helped me try it on.

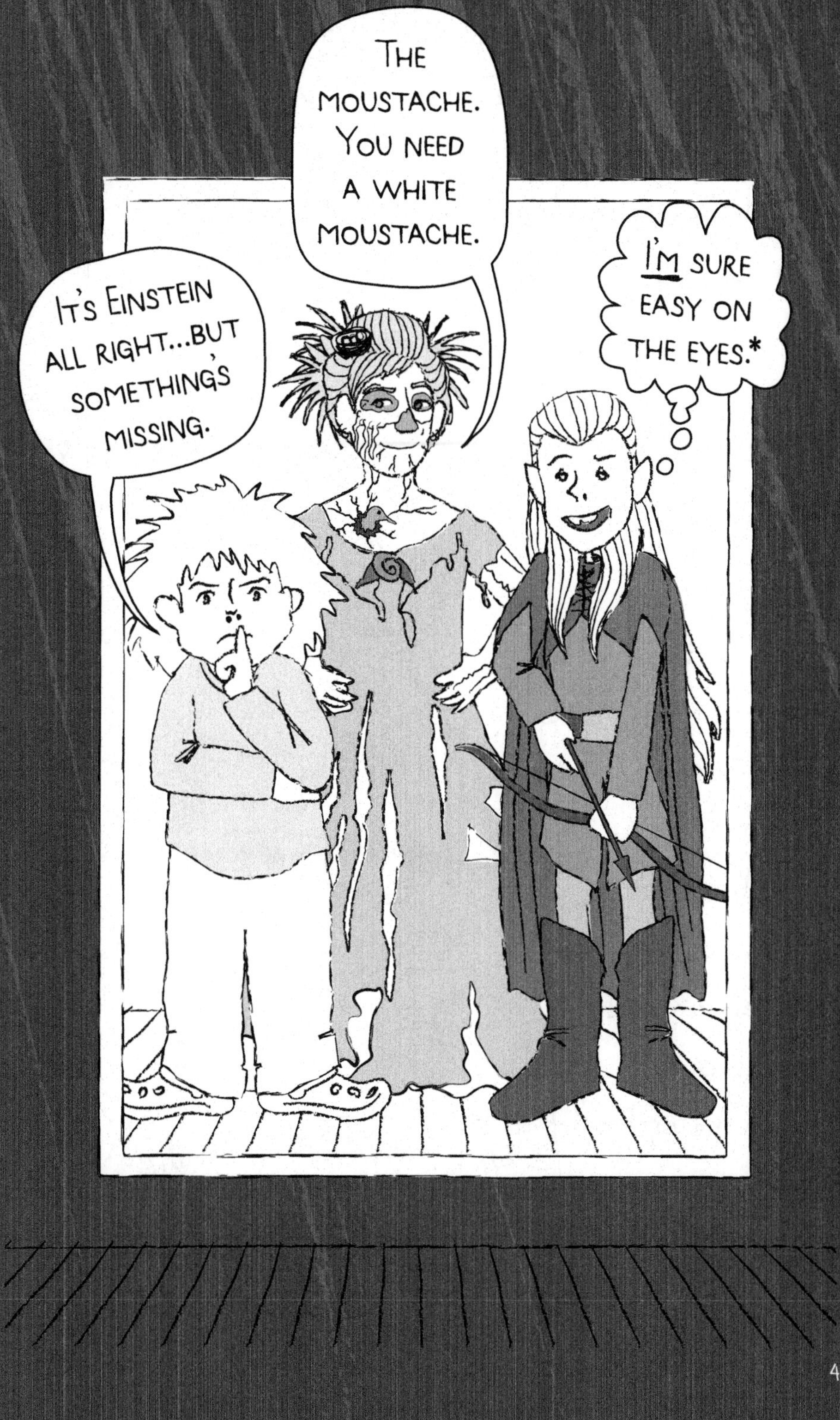
It's Einstein all right...but something's missing.
The moustache. You need a white moustache.
I'm sure easy on the eyes.*

Then she helped me find just the right moustache and showed me how to use this weird gluey stuff to stick it to my face. She said I should wear an old suit jacket of my dad's and a fat tie and bam, I'd be Einstein.

(Little does she know that I'm basically already an Einstein, what with the 6 A's on my report card and all.)

Before we left the costume store, Dad got inspired by all the wig-trying-on and picked out a costume of his own.

RHYTHM IS SOMETHING YOU EITHER HAVE OR DON'T HAVE...BUT WHEN YOU HAVE IT, YOU HAVE IT ALL OVER, BABY!

12 DAYS TILL HALLOWEEN! (GOOD THING I HAVE JACK, OR I'D HAVE TO TRICK-OR-TREAT WITH ELVIS.)

EXPERIMENT #1: IRON MAN

I started working on my Einstein project.

To get in the mood, I put on my costume and looked at some sciencey websites that showed physics experiments you can do at home! Here's the one I tried tonight:

WHAT YOU NEED

- 2 cups of cereal—the gross kind that has 100% of your daily vitamins (I used Total.)
- ½ cup of water
- a blender
- a super-strong magnet, like this:

Put the cereal and water in the blender and blend the cereal till it's a goopy mess. Pour the goop into a bowl and let it sit for 10 minutes. Then stick the magnet into the goop and stir it around. Little bits of iron stick to the magnet!

WHAT I LEARNED

Cereal that's good for you has weird stuff in it. Eat junk cereal instead. Also, dogs enjoy the goopy cereal when you're done with it, especially if you sprinkle bacon bits on top.

BUGLE BOY

Today I went with Jack's family to a town in the mountains called Estes Park. It's only about an hour from where we live.

Estes Park is famous because it's where Rocky Mountain National Park is. In case you've never been to a national park, I'll make a list of what you can expect to see when you go to one:

- ground
- rocks
- bushes
- trees
- more trees
- a couple of animals

So EXCITING! (NOT)

That's pretty much it.

OK, maybe you guessed that Rocky Mountain National Park has one other thing: mountains that are rocky. They're really tall mountains too—so tall that they have snow on top of them even in the summer.

So there I was in the car with Jack, Jack's grandpa, and Jack's mom, who was driving. Jack's mom was chattering away in Spanish to Abuelo in the front seat, and Jack was chattering away to me in English in the back seat. You may remember that Jack is a rock hound, so he gets excited about telling the epic* tale of how the mountains were made by sedimentary rock getting smashed into metamorphic rock over a couple billion years blah, blah, blah.

Still, I felt elated* because a) it wasn't a school day, and b) I was just a kid hanging out with his best friend and his Gameboy. (Oh, and Mrs. Lopez passed me a tin of those amazing cheese cookies she makes.)

In the autumn, people don't really go to Rocky Mountain National Park to see the mountains, though. They go to see the elk. Elk are like giant deer, and October happens to be the month when they get together for their annual elk conference.

So Mrs. Lopez parked the car near a really big meadow where hundreds or millions of elk were chillaxing in the drizzling rain. The four of us joined the crowd of humans eyeballing* the elk, who were eating grass and paying us no attention whatsoever.

"C'mon, let's bring Abuelo to the front so he can see better," Jack said to me, and he took his grandfather's hand.

"That's a delightful idea and all...but it's raining, and these elk are boring. I think I'll go back to the car and finish my Pokémon Emerald game..."

"¡Venga!" said Abuelo. I jumped. It was the first time I'd heard him speak, and his voice was surprisingly forceful.

"He says c'mon," said Jack.

So we made our way through the crowd. Turns out when you have a really old codger with you, people smile at you and are actually happy to give you cuts.

It was just starting to get dusky. Jack and Abuelo and I were sitting on a log, watching the elk mill around. I kept stealing peeks at Abuelo in the fading light. He wasn't talking anymore, and his eyes were drooping closed now and then. What was going on in that combed head of his? Was this quiet thing an act? Was he really a secret-agent scientist?

DO YOU THINK IT'S GOING TO RAIN AT ECOWEEK TOO?

I HOPE NOT. BUT IT'S ONLY 4 DAYS AWAY.

Just then, the dad elks—the ones with the big antlers—started causing a commotion. They lowered their heads and made this loud screeching noise like my trumpet makes when I'm trying to play a high E but can't hit the note right. In fact, the sound they make is called bugling (as in "bugle," not "bug," like it looks). Bugling is supposed to make the mom elks like them.

Next thing I knew, 2 of the dad elks were facing each other and pawing at the muddy ground. Then they bugled, dipped their heads down, and ran full-speed—right at each other! Their antlers crashed together, and then it was like an epic stick fight, only with big stick bouquets tied to the tops of their heads.

"Whoa," I said to Jack.

"Qué chido," Jack said to me.

And we fist-bumped over the top of Abuelo's little raisiny noggin. All in all, an exceptionally good day.

HEY, LADIES! LOOK OVER HERE! I'M QUITE EXQUISITE.*

ELEFANTE ESTÚPIDO

My evil Spanish teacher, Señor Espinoza

MWAH HA HA HA!

A+

$$$!

Remember how my mom got all conniptiony about the D on my report card, and how Jack was assigned to be my partner in Spanish class? Welp, Mom called my Spanish teacher to find out how I could do better, and he said, "Have Arnaldo practice with Joaquín at home."

Uh, yeah. Señor Espinoza assigned us Spanish names in his class. I'm Arnaldo and Jack is Joaquín. Just one example of his cruelty.

So without even getting my permission, Mom asked Jack if he would tutor me for 2 bucks an hour. He said he would tutor me <u>and</u> get me to exercise at the same time for 2 bucks an hour. (Why? Because he's a parents' pet, that's why.)

"Excelente!" my mom reportedly replied to Jack's Spanish/exercise combo idea.

"Unexcelente!" I said to her when she told me the plan. "I'm not doing it!"

"Oh good," she said. "The thrift store will be thrilled about the donation of your Xbox."

Which is how I came to be playing Spanish Elephant Tag with Jack, Bee, and Vivi at Jack's house after school today.

Jack basically invented this game where the person who's "it" has to hold his right ear with his left arm, then stick his right arm on the inside of his left elbow. The right, sticking-out arm is the elephant's trunk. When the elephant catches someone else, it's their turn to be "it."

TRY IT! IT'S EXCRUCIATINGLY* UNCOMFORTABLE.

55

As if that wasn't bad enough...when the elephant is just about to tag someone, that person shouts out a word from Señor Espinoza's vocabulary list.

If the elephant doesn't know the English equivalent,* he has to keep being the elephant. Guess who was the stupid elephant for the entire game.

57

First I have to run for science, and now I have to run for Spanish?! What is this, some giant conspiracy to turn every subject into P.E.?!

It was raining outside—what's new—so we had to play the game inside. Jack's abuelo sat with Slate in his lap and pretended to snooze. He also had a pad of paper and a pen in his hand, and I noticed that once in a while he'd wake up and write something down. I'm guessing he's involved in a clandestine project he can't tell anyone about...

AM I SLEEPING? OR AM I DREAMING UP A DANGEROUS NEW INVENTION?

A BELCH IS BUT A GUST OF WIND THAT COMETH FROM THE HEART, BUT SHOULD IT TAKE A DOWNWARD TREND, IT TURNETH TO A FART.

HEART OF DARKNESS

Oh my gosh. I can hardly believe I'm still alive to tell this tale.

It all started when the thunder woke me up again in the middle of the night. On my way to the bathroom, I looked out my window and there he was...the person with the black umbrella, standing in the rain in a pool of light under the streetlamp.

I gasped and covered my mouth with my hands, because for some reason that's what you do when you gasp. (Try it right now. You'll see what I mean.) My fingers felt something furry, and that's when I realized I'd fallen asleep with my Einstein wig and moustache on.

All of a sudden I had a compelling urge to go see what Mr. Mot (or whoever this was) was up to. Aldo Zelnick might not have had enough courage to go find out, but Albert Einstein was a pretty audacious guy. So before I could change my mind, I tiptoed downstairs, pulled on my rain boots, grabbed a coat and umbrella, and stepped out into the storm, closing the door silently behind me. (Sneaking out in the middle of the night is frowned upon in the Zelnick house. Especially for 10-year-olds. So I had to be quiet.)

By now the mystery man's umbrella was bobbing away from me down the street. It was uber dark out, but the streetlight and flashes of lightning made it so I could kinda keep him in sight. I gulped and set off after him, ducking behind cars and trees and bushes so that if he looked back, he wouldn't see me following him. I mean, even if it <u>was</u> Mr. Mot, he was probably doing something sneaky that he wouldn't want me to see.

WHAT AM I, CRAZY?! THESE ARE OBVIOUSLY THE EXACT RIGHT CONDITIONS FOR A DEMENTOR OR ZOMBIE ATTACK. BUT SOMEHOW EINSTEIN-ME FEELS CURIOUS INSTEAD OF APPREHENSIVE.

Umbrella guy moved slowly but steadily. I'd followed him for about a block when, as he was passing by our fort tree, lightning popped and I caught a glimpse of bright pink below his black umbrella. I snuck closer—just a few trees away now—but when the lightning flickered again, he was gone.

I splashed ahead, searching, but the lightning had diminished and I couldn't see anything. I stopped to catch my breath, which in the cold dampness was coming out of my mouth in little smoke-like puffs.

Einstein-me got all entranced* by my dragon-like ability to breathe smoke. But then Aldo-me noticed round, yellow eyes glowing in the darkness. They looked like two small moons—and they were coming toward me! *That's not Mr. Mot!* I thought.

Even Einstein-me wigged out at that point. I dropped the umbrella and ran home faster than the speed of light. I managed to sneak into my house without my parents noticing, and now I'm back in my bedroom, talking to myself in the mirror to calm myself down.

In case you're wondering, here's what Einstein looks like when he's freaked and dripping wet:

THE FELLOWSHIP IS BREAKING

Bee and Jack met me at the fort after school today so I could tell them what happened last night.

Besides being all hidden and secret, the amazing thing about our fort under the giant pine tree is that the ground stays dry. So it's the one place outside (I mostly hate OUTSIDE) that's good for hanging out, even during bad weather.

Bee brought a little baggie of eggplant* chips to share. They're kinda like potato chips, only they're made from eggplants from Bee's garden.

So in between mouthfuls I described the guy with the black umbrella and how I followed him in the darkness.

EGGPLANT CHIPS = NOT BAD. THIS IS HOW ALL VEGGIES SHOULD BE SERVED: OILED, SALTED, AND CRISPY, DONTCHA THINK?

I LIVE TO BE SERVED.

"At first I thought it was Mr. Mot, but it turned out to be something creepier," I said.

"Probably a gray wizard," decided Jack.

"Oh c'mon. It's just someone who likes to go for walks at night!" said Bee.

"In the rain?" I said. "And what about the yellow eyes?"

"Werewolf," shrugged Jack. "Or goblin. Maybe vampire."

"That's what I think!" I said. "Like, it's a ghoul or something."

"You're imagining things, silly," said Bee. "Lots of people go for walks in the rain. And the yellow 'eyes' were probably just car headlights coming down the street."

"Well, creatures of evil are called to roam the earth as Halloween approaches...," added Jack, "and Halloween is just 10 days away!"

"Don't be absurd," said Bee. "And which one of you has been leaving trash in our fort?" She pointed at a banana peel on the ground and an empty Eggo waffle box wedged in the knot of the tree.

"Not me!" I said. "My mom only buys dumb organic waffles."

"I don't like bananas or waffles," said Jack. "And instead of arguing, we should be talking about EcoWeek...or practicing our Spanish."

"Oh good!" said Bee. "Let's practice!"

"Oh good!" I mimicked. "Let's not and say we did!"

"But we have a test in Señor Espinoza's class tomorrow, Aldo," said Jack. "I'm sure you can get an A if we practice for just a couple minutes."

"Spanish is the worst!" I exploded. "Your brain learned it when it was a baby. My brain got too Englished by now or something. It must have anti-Español* force fields set up around it because Nothing's. Getting. Through." I could feel my cheeks turn cherry-Slushie red and my eyes burning. Jack was looking down at the ground, drawing in the dirt with a stick. For some reason that made me even angrier. "You just want to make 2 bucks!" I added. "And besides, nobody needs to know how to speak Spanish because THE WHOLE WORLD SPEAKS ENGLISH!!!"

Jack pressed his eyes with his palms, then crawled out of the fort without saying a word. Slate followed him, leaving a trail of toots behind.

"You hurt his feelings, Aldo," said Bee. "Go tell him you're sorry."

"That's a girl thing. He's fine. He probably just wanted to go home and eat a peanut butter sandwich."

"He's not fine. You yelled at him."

"I didn't yell. That was just...loud saying. Besides, Jack and I have been best friends since before we were born. I know when he's fine. He's fine."

"This time's different, Aldo," she said. Then she crawled out too.

I sighed and leaned back against the tree trunk. Don't Jack and Bee know that forts are supposed to be for fun and adventure (and snacks)? Not for talking about homework and "feelings." Sheesh.

la práctica hace al maestro

67

DAM
TROUBLE

This morning I stopped at Jack's house on the walk to school, like I always do, but he wasn't there!

"He left a couple minutes ago," said Mrs. Lopez. She and Abuelo were sitting at the kitchen table.

"Oh. OK...," I said. "He must have had to get to class early for some reason."

Abuelo was smiling at me and stirring his coffee with a spoon. Then he stopped stirring and stuck the wet spoon into his shirt pocket.

"Abuelo likes you, Aldo," said Mrs. Lopez.

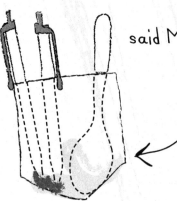

COULD THIS BE THE <u>REAL</u> REASON ALL BRAINIACS USE POCKET PROTECTORS?

"Uh, gotta get to school," I said. "*Adios, muchacho.*" Ack. That wasn't the right thing to say, but it was the only phrase I could remember from Spanish class about how to say goodbye.

Still grinning at me, Abuelo lifted his left pointer finger and tapped the side of his nose with it, twice. Danny taught me that gesture. It's not really sign language, but it means, "We have a secret, you and me."

TAP!
TAP!

Weird! I thought. *Does he know that I know that he might still be doing secret science?* I turned and hurried back out into the rainy morning.

I found Jack on the playground with Danny. But when I tried to talk to Jack, he acted like he couldn't hear me...and we all know that Danny, the deaf kid, couldn't hear me. So I just stood there and watched them play tetherball. In the rain.

Jack ignored me all day at school. At lunch he sat on the opposite end of the long table as me. Then when it was time to walk home, Jack crossed to the other side of the street from the one we usually walk on and sprinted ahead. He knows I don't sprint.

That's when I started to think Bee might actually be right: *Jack is annoyed with me!*

Speaking of Bee, she was standing near the bent stop sign, waiting for me.

"Jack's mad, huh," she said.

"I guess."

The rain was rushing down the gutter next to the curb, creating a miniature river. I picked up a twig and dropped it into the current. Bee and I watched it float downstream till it disappeared into the storm grate.

Even though she's basically a girl, Bee has
decent construction instincts. She grabbed a few
big stones and plopped them into the water. They
were heavy enough that the rainwater didn't wash
them away.

We had ourselves the beginning of a dam!

We rushed to get more rocks
and sticks to make a dam big and
strong enough to hold back the gutter-river.

Then I noticed Jack standing on the
street corner cattywampus from the one
we were working on. He was with another
kid, and THEY were making a gutter-dam.
It was Tommy Geller, my former archenemy
(who later turned out to be a good guy) from
Dana Elementary. He's in 6th grade this year, at
the middle school.

"Let's go see if they want to build a dam with us," suggested Bee.

"Nah," I said. "They can come over here if they want to." Inside me I could feel a microscopic electron of sadness whizzing around. It was bothering all the happy particles from my day, like the pepperoni pizza atoms from lunch and the ego* atoms from history class because I got back my European Expansion test with a big A+ marked on the top.

But that made me think of something I read that Einstein said: "If you want to live a happy life, tie it to a goal, not to people or things." So I focused on the goal of helping Bee build the most awesome dam our neighborhood's gutters had ever seen.

We added more and more rocks and pine cones and leaves, until the water was starting to spill out of the gutter and into the street. I could see that Jack and Tommy were doing the same thing on their corner. At this rate, the entire intersection would be underwater in no time.

"This is awesome!" I yelled to no one in particular.

But Bee the buzzkiller didn't agree. "I don't think we should flood the street, Aldo," she said.

"Aw, don't be such a partypooper. We're just experimenting with water energy! It's practically science homework!"

LOVE DAMS. HATE GETTING IN TROUBLE.

Jack and Tommy were now skateboarding through the mini-lake. Rooster-tail sprays of water shot up behind them as they glided. It kinda looked like they were waterskiing.

Meanwhile, Bee was demolishing our dam rock by rock, stick by stick, and the rainwater was again flowing down the gutter on our side of the street.

"I'm outta here," I said to Bee. And I turned and slogged home in the rain, leaving my so-called friends to have their H_2O hijinks without me.

I CAN'T SKATEBOARD! I'M TERRIBLE AT ANYTHING WHERE I HAVE TO BALANCE AND MOVE AT THE SAME TIME.

Oh, and also, I got a D on today's Spanish test. So life's just *bueno*.

EXPERIMENT #2: ELECTRIC MAX

- 1 cat or fuzzy object
- carpeted floor in a dark room

Nicely rub your cat around on the carpet. I don't have a cat, so I used Max. If you don't have a cat or a Max, use a fuzzy blanket or stuffed animal.

The science website says that when different materials rub against each other, one might want the other's electrons and pull them away. When the electrons fly through the air, that's static electricity. In a dark room, you can actually see the sparks! Zap!

WHAT I LEARNED

Dogs can be hard to pull around when they don't want to be.

FIRST OF ALL, I AM NOT A 'MATERIAL.' SECOND OF ALL, I LIKE MY ELECTRONS JUST THE WAY THEY ARE, THANK YOU VERY MUCH.

THE GREAT DIVIDE

I'M 100% NATURAL AND AN ESSENTIAL PART OF THE FOOD CHAIN.

I'M 100% DELICIOUS AND AVAILABLE IN REGULAR OR SOUR.

GUMMI

EcoWeek starts tomorrow! All us 5th graders and a few of the teachers will take a bus to a camp in the mountains near the Continental Divide, a.k.a. the Great Divide. It's the highest ridge down the top of the Rocky Mountains, where if you fell off the west side, you'd roll to California and into the Pacific Ocean, and if you fell off the east side, you'd roll to New Orleans and the Gulf of Mexico.

THIS IS COOL: WHENEVER IT RAINS OR SNOWS ON THE ROCKIES, ALL THE DROPS OF WATER THAT LAND ON THIS SIDE OF THE MOUNTAINS ROLL DOWNHILL TO THE EAST...

...AND THE DROPS ON THIS SIDE ROLL DOWN TO THE WEST!

I don't know why the trip is called EcoWeek, though, because it's just 2 nights and 3 days (hello!).

Now, you know me; I'm not a big camping enthusiast.* But at EcoWeek, you don't sleep in a tent on the cold, rocky ground or eat food you roast on sticks. Instead, you get a real bed inside a real building, and real meals in a real cafeteria. Best of all, you get to go with your friends, so it's basically a 56-hour sleepover marathon.

Anyway, we're leaving for camp tomorrow, so tonight I'm packing all the essentials* on the list Mr. Krug gave us, like a sleeping

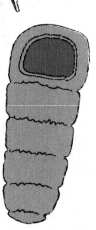

bag and footy pajamas. Jack
and I have been looking
forward to EcoWeek ever
since kindergarten. He's still
avoiding me, though. Geez,
if he doesn't get a better
attitude, he's not gonna
enjoy the trip one
bit.

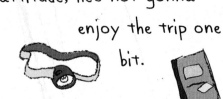

ECOWEEK DAY 1:

Today we got to ride in a big yellow school bus to the camp. I sat next to Danny, and we played hangman the whole way. Toward the end of the trip the roads were pretty squiggly, but only one kid got bus-sick. It was Emilio. After he threw up, I passed him my gummy worms because gummy worms always make me feel better, but for some reason he didn't want any.

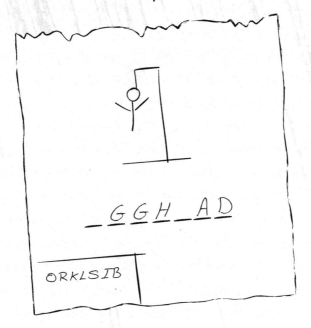

_ G G H _ A D

ORKLSIB

When we got to the camp, we carried our stuff into the dorms. There's one wing of rooms for the boys and another wing for the girls, with 2 sets of bunkbeds in each room. My room has me, Danny, Emilio, and Marvin Shoemaker. I picked a bottom bunk because: no climbing!

BUNK SWEET BUNK.
(LOOKS LIKE THE BEST ONE, DONTCHA THINK?)

But unfortunately, there <u>was</u> climbing in the afternoon because the rain took the afternoon off and we were able to do the Ropes Course. The Ropes Course is like a circus act for kids who have no circus experience. One at a time you climb up a tall pole, then you walk across the catwalk, which sounds glamorous but is really just a horizontal log way high off the ground.

Remember how I'm terrible at activities where you have to balance and move at the same time? Yeah. I'm probably the least catlike kid on Earth, so it shouldn't come as a surprise that I <u>fell off the catwalk.</u> Luckily the harness and rope I was tied to caught me, but still, it's embarrassing dangling in the air like a worm on the end of a fishing line!

(Bee, on the other hand, loves to climb really tall things and thought the catwalk was the cat's pajamas. She practically ran across it. Show-off.)

BEE IS THE MOST CATLIKE KID I KNOW. (YEAH, ISN'T IT WEIRD?)

Then, after an excellent dinner of chicken parmesan (which Jack won't eat so he got a peanut butter sandwich, I noticed), we all gathered in the rain around a tiny, smoky campfire...to sing. Because apparently that's what you do around campfires—sing silly songs about baby sharks and boom-chicka-booms and stuff like that. I sat by Danny again. He likes music, and he's good at the hand motions that go with songs. Jack picked a sitting log on the opposite side of the fire from me and pretended to be having fun with Sawyer and Jay. They're just random kids in our class.

EUREKA!* LOOK AT SEÑOR ESPINOZA! HE LOOKS JUST LIKE THE GHOUL MAN I SAW IN OUR NEIGHBORHOOD!

Before we went to bed, one of the camp counselors told us the tale of Stumpy, the ghost who haunts the camp. He's called that because he has a peg-leg, and supposedly you can hear him stomping down the halls in the middle of the night. Even though it's only 8 days till Halloween, I'm not scared of Stumpy. Now that I noticed Señor Espinoza looks like the mystery man, I'm way more apprehensive about what <u>he</u> might be up to.

There. I just leaned a chair up under the doorknob into our room, like they do in the movies. That should keep out any intruders.

I'm in my bed writing this. It's lights out, so I'm using the trusty headlamp Jack lent me when I went to Minnesota this summer—Jack, who right now is zipped into a sleeping bag a few rooms away from me instead of dangling over the edge of the top bunk to talk to me in the dark, like I always imagined.

START ✗ ⋯⋯⋯ ✗ END?
IF ONLY. Now
WE HIKE <u>BACK</u>.

ECOWEEK DAY 2:

I guess I survived the night because next thing I knew, our teachers were waking us up. It was 6 a.m. and still dark! But at least we got French toast and the most exquisite breakfast meat known to man—bacon. Then the cafeteria people set out a bunch of bread and ham and cheese and stuff so we could pack our own lunches for today's hike.

Yes, the appalling "h" word. Hike is just a euphemism* for "walking uphill." I mean, I guess the mountains are OK-looking, but I'll never understand why people feel the need to walk up them.

At least we got to choose: a short hike to a meadow; a medium hike to an old crashed airplane; or a long hike to the mountain top. Bee and Danny picked the long hike, of course. I didn't wanna seem like a baby, plus the crashed plane was kinda enticing,* so I chose medium.

As luck would have it, Señor Espinoza led the medium hike. He didn't look so dastardly in the light of day, though. Jack and Emilio clumped into the medium group too. The 3 of them started talking Spanish as we set off. Whatever they were saying must have been pretty hilarious, because Jack kept laughing so hard I thought for sure he was gonna pee his cargo pants. (I am not even exaggerating.* One time in kindergarten I accidentally sneezed a booger onto our teacher, Miss Sparkel, and Jack cracked up so hard that yup, he soaked his SpongeBob shorts.)

So I couldn't understand their Spanish jokes...so what? I was too out-of-breath to laugh anyway. This hike was definitely one of those times when medium actually means extreme—like when you pick medium at the salsa bar and it burns your tastebuds off. The trail had some flat parts, where you could just walk along and pretend to be enjoying the rain-soaked scenery, la-di-da, but there were super-steep sections, too, where your legs and lungs let you know they really did <u>not</u> appreciate the lack of oxygen atoms at this high altitude.

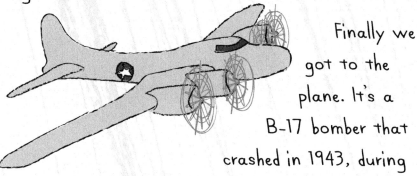

Finally we got to the plane. It's a B-17 bomber that crashed in 1943, during World War 2. Mr. Krug explained that it happened at night, in the dark. The crew had gotten mixed up about their location and the plane was flying too low. A million chunks of metal still lie scattered all over the boulder field.

All the laughing and talking stopped as we imagined what it must have been like when the giant airplane smashed into the mountainside that night. 10 army guys were on board. 4 of them died.

PEACE CANNOT BE KEPT BY FORCE. IT CAN ONLY BE ACHIEVED BY UNDERSTANDING.
- ALBERT EINSTEIN

Geez. I never knew anything in World War 2 happened where I live. I did know that Einstein and Abuelo were part of that old war. The library books I read about Einstein made it sound like the wartime science stuff and secret laboratories and atomic bombs were kinda exciting. But today there was a crashed warplane right in front of me, and all I felt was atomic sadness.

After dinner we looked through telescopes at the cloudy sky and made bead bracelets. Well actually, Bee made bead bracelets while Danny and I tried to see how many beads we could balance on our noses. The record: 2.

While we were beading, Bee brought up Halloween. "Do you want to go trick-or-treating with me, Aldo?" she asked.

"I always go with Jack," I said.

"I know...but I thought maybe Jack had other plans this year."

"Whaddya mean, 'other plans?'"

"I mean, he told me he might go trick-or-treating with Tommy Geller."

"Oh. That's dumb."

"Maybe <u>Danny</u> could come with us!" exclaimed Bee, and she asked him in sign language.

Danny said yes. So it's looking like Halloween is gonna be strange this year. Strange as in Jackless. Hard to imagine, really.

At bedtime I fell asleep instantly because of exhaustion from the hike. But then I woke up a minute ago to a clump, clump, clumping noise coming from the hallway outside our door!

Emilio was in the bottom bunk across from me. "Emilio, wake up!" I loud-whispered. "Do you hear that?"

"It's just someone walking to the bathroom," he whispered back.

Good thing I stuck the chair under the doorknob again, I thought. But then Emilio's bathroom suggestion egged on* my bladder and I realized I had to go—immediately!

"Emilio, come to the bathroom with me!"

"No way. I'm sleeping."

"Please? Pretty please with gummy worms on top? I actually do have some gummy worms left! You can have them!"

"Zelnick, you're such an infant. Oh all right."

So Emilio and I ran down the hallway to the bathroom, speed-peed, then were starting to run back when a giant crack of thunder encouraged us to bolt even faster. And even though we didn't see a ghost, I might have screamed.
Just a little.

SO YOU'RE SAYIN' YOU'RE GLAD YOU PACKED ME AFTER ALL? I THOUGHT SO.

ECOWEEK DAY 3:

Up again at 6 a.m. During the morning we played in a stream and walked around some mostly-crumbled buildings from the olden days, when the camp used to be a ranch and a cemetery.

(Yes, we camped near an old cemetery. Glad I didn't know <u>that</u> the last 2 nights.)

I picked up a little brown rock with black flecks I noticed near one of the old headstones. Jack was hanging out with Jay and Sawyer again. I walked over to them and held out the rock in the palm of my hand.

"This looks like a good one," I said, and I offered it to Jack.

"It looks like a rock," laughed Jay, and he bumped my hand from underneath, which made the rock go flying off into the bushes.

POW!!!

Danny saw what happened and started sign-languaging angrily at Jay, which made Jay and Sawyer laugh even harder. And don't think Jack wasn't laughing too, because he was.

That electron of sadness started whizzing around inside me again, only this time it was getting more forceful.

"¡Basta!" said Señor Espinoza. "Enough is enough,* boys. It's time to get back to the dorms and load up your things."

So that's how EcoWeek ended. We climbed onto the bus and drove back to Dana Elementary.

Tonight I'm home in my own bed with real covers and Max. It's raining again and thundering, but still, it's cozy and safe here. No catwalks. No plane crashes. No friend problems.

And no ghosts. Oh yeah. Except the ghoul with the yellow eyes who haunts our neighborhood and is trying to get me. Could it be Señor Espinoza?

ESKIMO SCRABBLE

Mr. Mot and Bee dropped by after dinner today. It seemed strange that they would come together, but they brought a box of Eskimo Pies,* which distracted me. They asked me and my dad if we wanted to join them in a game of Scrabble.

"Definitely!" said Dad, but then Mr. Mot started talking to him about some guitar stuff, and Bee started talking to me about *A Wrinkle in Time*, and precious minutes were ticking by.

"Enough of this chit-chat," I had to say. "It's warm in here, and the Eskimo Pies are endangered.*"

So we nibbled on chocolate-covered-ice-cream-on-a-stick, sipped the cinnamon tea my dad brought to the table, and were enjoying a bodacious game of Scrabble when I noticed Bee giving Mr. Mot big-eyeball looks. You know, the sneaky kind that mean, "It's time to do that thing we talked about!"

Mr. Mot cleared his throat and asked, "So Aldo, am I to understand that you and the amiable Jack are crossing swords?"

"What?" I said. "If you mean for Halloween, Jack has a bow and arrow and I have an axe dealie...but I'm not going to use it this year. We don't have swords."

"'Crossing swords' means arguing, Aldo," said Dad. "Is there a problem between you and Jack?"

"Oh." I glared at Bee, who didn't notice because she was busy playing the word FRIEND on the Scrabble board. "It's no big deal. Jack just keeps trying to teach me Spanish and I don't care about Spanish, that's all."

"Your mom asked Jack to help you in Spanish, didn't she?" said Dad.

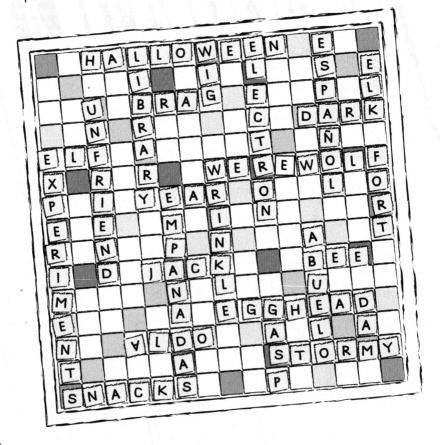

"Yeah, but it doesn't work for your friend to be your teacher," I said as I added the letters U and N on top of Bee's FRIEND. "Besides, I'm just <u>bad</u> at other languages." I picked up my tea and took a slurp. "So...how 'bout all this rain we've been having?"

"Ahhh," said Mr. Mot. "The alluring ineptitude excuse. One says one simply <u>cannot</u> do something rather than admit to oneself the truth: that one <u>chooses</u> not to try."

"I agree, Aldo," said Dad. "Spanish may be harder for you than other subjects, but you would do fine if you put in the effort. If your attitude about Spanish is coming between you and the guy who's been your best friend since you were both in diapers, though, then that's an even bigger concern."

"Not only that," said Mr. Mot, "but I read an interesting article in today's newspaper. The experts they interviewed said that within 20 years, more than half of all Americans will speak Español <u>as their first language.</u> Just like Jack's family."

I looked around the table at the 3 eager*
faces looking back at me and sighed. "Oh all right,"
I said. "I'll try harder in Spanish, and I'll tell Jack
I'm sorry. Happy?"

"Yay!" said Bee.

"Good man," said Dad.

"Learn from yesterday, live for today, hope
for tomorrow," said Mr. Mot.

"Whatever. I'm going to bed," I said. And
I grabbed my copy of A Wrinkle in Time and
stomped up the stairs to my room.

"Bogus," I said to my betta fish, peaceful and
alone in his bowl, "you don't know how good you
have it."

HARD TO SAY I'M SORRY

This morning in Spanish class, I decided to apologize to Jack, I mean Joaquín. Since we're partners, we sit together at the same table.

"Today we're going to work on common phrases you would need to travel in a Spanish-speaking country," said Señor Espinoza, who was wearing a bright pink shirt under his usual gray sweater-vest. "Get out your textbooks and turn to page 67..."

"I think Señor Espinoza is the ghoul man!"
I whispered to Jack. "He's evil, plus he's got the
right kind of coat and hat, plus I remember seeing
pink that night I snuck out of the house to follow
him, plus he's out to get me!"

"In case you haven't noticed, I'm not talking
to you," Jack whispered back.

"Oh all right... My dad says I have to tell
you sorry."

"Now," announced Señor Espinoza to the
class, "let's say 'I'm hungry.' Tengo hambre. Repeat
after me, please. Tengo hambre."

"Your dad says to say you're sorry?" Jack whispered back to me.

"Oh, well actually Mr. Mot and Bee and my dad all said I have to say sorry. So, here goes: I'm sorry I'm not good at Spanish."

"Now, class," said Senor Espinoza, "here's an important one: 'Where's the bathroom?' is ¿Donde está el cuarto de baño? Repeat after me: ¿Donde está el cuarto de baño?"

"I don't care if you're good at Spanish, Aldo," whispered Jack. "But you make it seem like it's wrong to speak Spanish."

"It's not wrong, exactly...It's just confusing to have 2 languages going on at the same time."

"Well it's confusing for people who speak Spanish to try to understand English."

"But English is still the main language!"

"Now," said Senor Espinoza, "let's say, 'I don't understand.' No entiendo. Repeat after me, class. No entiendo."

"*No entiendo*," I repeated out loud, then I whispered, "Jack, I said I'm sorry."

"Say it in Spanish then," Jack hissed.

"I don't know how to. And that's a dumb thing to expect!"

"Now, class, let's say, 'I'm lost,' said Señor Espinoza. "*Estoy perdido.* Repeat after me, please. *Estoy perdido.*"

"I'm lost," I said.

Jack shook his head, crossed his arms across his chest, and started ignoring me again. Then later in the day, we had band class together. Jack sits behind me, and today he kept accidentally on purpose poking me with his trombone. Fine. See if I care. He'll be sorry when Señor Espinoza turns into a werewolf or kidnaps me or eats all the trick-or-treaters on Halloween night...or whatever his evil plans are.

EXPERIMENT #3: BALLOON IN A BOTTLE

WHAT YOU NEED

- 1 small balloon
- 1 16-ounce glass bottle
- 1 tablespoon of water
- An oven mitt

CAUTION: HOT!

Put the water into the empty bottle, then put the bottle in the microwave. Microwave on high until the water boils and is almost gone. At this point the bottle will be full of steam and VERY HOT. Put on the oven mitt and take the bottle out of the microwave. Stretch the mouth of the balloon over the end of the bottle. Watch what happens to the balloon as the bottle cools off. It gets sucked into the bottle, and it even inflates upside-down inside the bottle!

WHAT I LEARNED

This experiment is a good excuse to tell your parents you need to drink a soda. Also, it has something to do with hot, wet air turning back into water as it cools off.

RAKE, RAKE

WHY, MY MAMA TAUGHT ME HOW TO WORK WHEN I WAS JUST A GARDEN FORK.

THAT WAS BACK WHEN THERE WEREN'T ANY CHILD LABOR LAWS.

Today after school my mom was in the backyard raking leaves, even though they're totally soggy from all the rain we've been having. She asked me to help her.

"I have to finish my Einstein report," I said. "It's due tomorrow! I don't have time to do both."

"Time is relative," said Mom with a wink, and she handed me a rake.

So there we were, raking in the rain. *Oh joy.*

"How's Spanish class going?" she asks.

"Bad. And Señor Espinoza is evil." Rake, rake.

"I've known him for many years, Aldo. He's a nice man." Rake, rake.

"His eyes glow in the dark. He's <u>after me!</u>" Hard rake, hard rake.

"Nobody's 'after' you. You're being ridiculous." Rake, rake. "But your dad and I do feel bad that you and Jack aren't getting along. Say, why don't we invite Jack over for dinner tonight! We could have cheese pizza. That's his favorite." Rake, rake.

Rake, rake. "No!" Rake, rake. Rake, rake.

Sniff, sniff. "Aldo, have you showered lately?"

"No. Good idea!" Drop rake. Run inside.

HUH. I GUESS I <u>CAN</u> SPRINT SOMETIMES.

After showering, having dinner, and catching up on a DVR'd episode of "Through the Wormhole with Morgan Freeman," I finished my Einstein report. It's all beautifully written on lined paper, with indented paragraphs and complete sentences and punctuation and everything. I even gave it a great title:

He Was an Einstein
(And So Am I)

by Aldo Zelnick

Then I placed the report safely in my backpack and had a stack of Oreos and a glass of milk to celebrate. The treat at the end is the best part of a project, wouldn't you agree?

And now, just for my sketchbook readers (which is me, and sometimes Jack and Bee and Mr. Mot), an Einstein quiz:

1. What year was Albert Einstein born?

   ☐ 1978
   ☐ 1879
   ☐ 1789

2. Where was Einstein born?

   ☐ England
   ☐ Germany
   ☐ New Jersey

3. Einstein discovered the photon, which is a:

   ☐ Bowl of Asian soup
   ☐ Ton of enemies
   ☐ Particle of light

4. Einstein stuck out his tongue in that famous photo because:

☐ He was at the doctor's office.

☐ He was gagging after accidentally eating vegetables.

☐ He was annoyed with paparazzi who were following him on his birthday.

5. After he died, Einstein's _____ was saved and studied by scientists.

☐ Brain

☐ Computer

☐ Notebook

I'm still wondering about Einstein's famous equation, though: e = mc². It turns out it means energy = mass times the speed of light squared. Mass is kinda like weight. And the speed of light is about 186,000 miles per second. If you "square" the speed of light, you multiply 186,000 times 186,000 (on a calculator!)...and you get about 34 million.

So does that mean my energy should equal my weight times 34 million? I'm kinda short for my weight, but still, that seems like <u>way</u> more energy than I actually have! I think some people (like me) just have less energy than other people (pretty much everyone else). Maybe that's what Einstein meant about everything being relative.

THE SCALES ARE TIPPING IN MY FAVOR, JACK!

YOU'VE ALWAYS HAD ME BEAT IN THE MASS DEPARTMENT, CUATE.

IS THIS WHAT THEY MEAN BY A NOBLE GAS?

Plus, all this stuff about things being made of little particles called atoms...it's kinda hard to believe, dontcha think? According to Einstein and *A Wrinkle in Time*, things that seem totally solid in real life, such as my kitchen table, actually have loads of microscopic holes in them.

And time, which I also think of as steady... tick, tick, tick...is just an illusion too. If you know how to wrinkle it, you can travel instantly to galaxies far away, hang out in space for a few days, then return—and arrive back on Earth before you left it!

Physics is creepy in an interesting sort of way. Like scary movies. And clowns. (Actually, clowns are just creepy.) Physics is more like...that eerie magician on TV, Criss Angel Mindfreak. No wonder Abuelo can't give it up.

CREEPY?!

Welp, it's 2 days till Halloween. I have a cool costume, I completed my Einstein report, and I finished *A Wrinkle in Time*. I'm almost ready—just jack o'lanterns to carve at Goosy's tomorrow night and a trick-or-treating plan to create with Bee and Danny.

My new Halloween goal is to get more candy than Jack. Now if it would just stop raining!

Q: How MANY EINSTEINS DOES IT
   TAKE TO CHANGE A LIGHTBULB?

I LOVE YOU
JUST THE WAY
YOU ARE.

A: THAT DEPENDS ON THE SPEED OF THE CHANGER AND THE MASS OF THE BULB. OR VICE VERSA, OF COURSE. THEN AGAIN, IT JUST MIGHT BE EASIER TO LEAVE THE BULB ALONE AND CHANGE THE ROOM. IT'S ALL RELATIVE.

BACON BOY IN
THE CENTER-CUT CLASSIC ADAPTATION OF
A WRINKLE IN TIME
HOLD TIGHT, C.W.! WE'RE TRAVELING THROUGH A WRINKLE IN TIME AND SPACE TO THE FAR-AWAY PLANET OF CAMAZOTZ! AN EVIL RULER THERE IS ABOUT TO DESTROY THE EARTH!
I HAVE BEEN WAITING FOR YOU, MY DEARS.
OH NO! VORACIO HAS BACONNAPPED MY FATHER! DON'T LOOK INTO VORACIO'S EYES, C.W. THEY'LL HYPNOTIZE YOU!
MY INITIALS MAY NOT STAND FOR CHARLES WALLACE, BUT I'M PLENTY COURAGEOUS TOO.

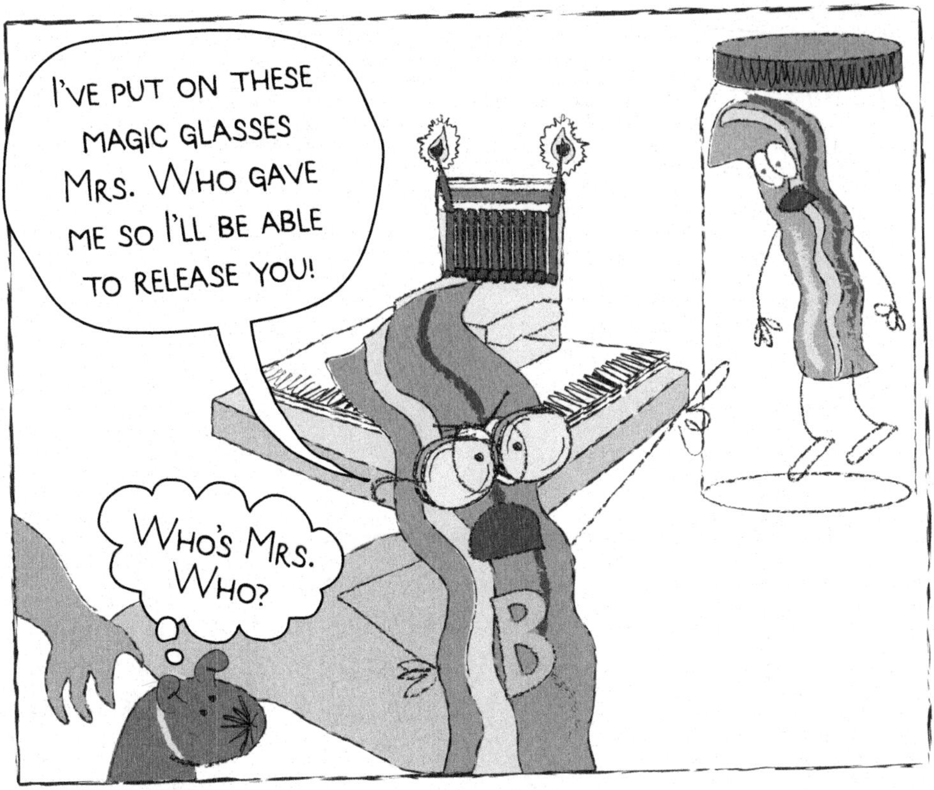
I'VE PUT ON THESE MAGIC GLASSES MRS. WHO GAVE ME SO I'LL BE ABLE TO RELEASE YOU!
WHO'S MRS. WHO?

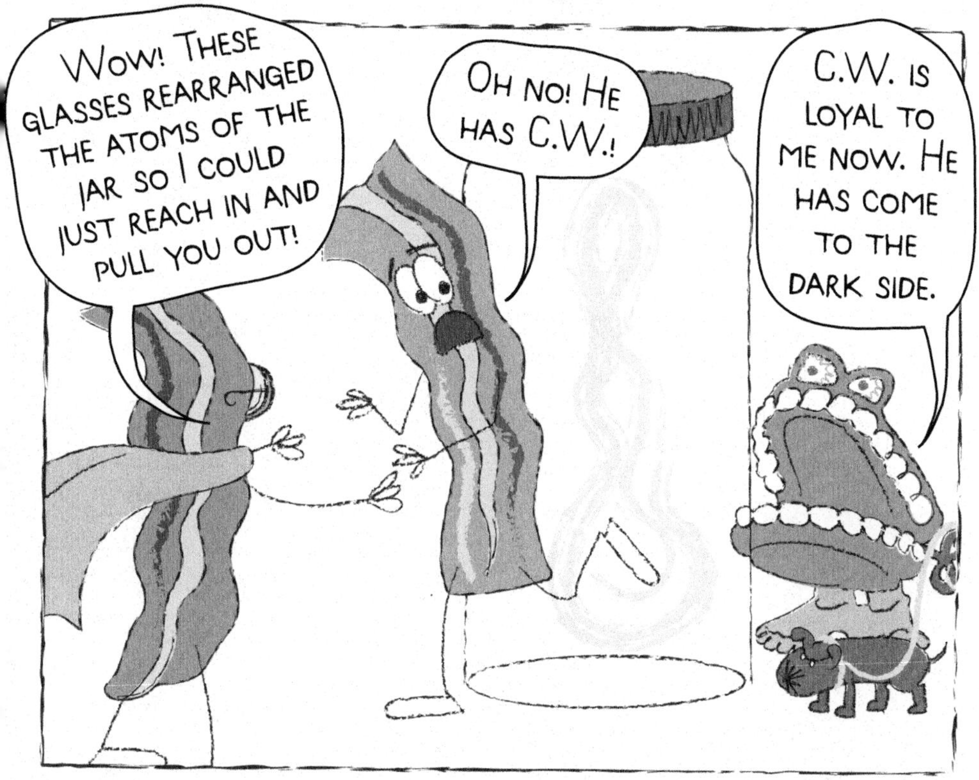
WOW! THESE GLASSES REARRANGED THE ATOMS OF THE JAR SO I COULD JUST REACH IN AND PULL YOU OUT!
OH NO! HE HAS C.W.!
C.W. IS LOYAL TO ME NOW. HE HAS COME TO THE DARK SIDE.

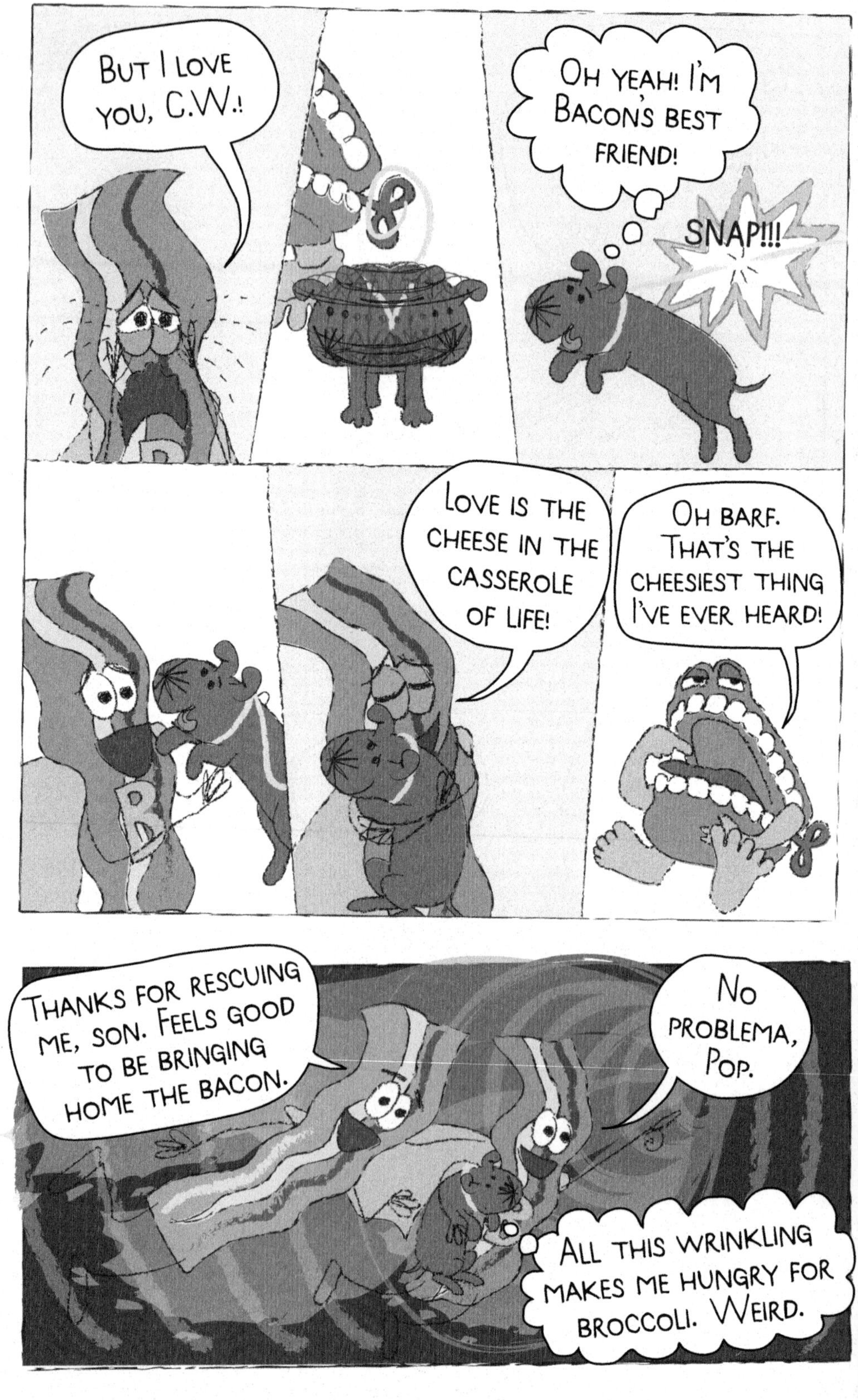

BUT I LOVE YOU, C.W.!
OH YEAH! I'M BACON'S BEST FRIEND!
SNAP!!!
LOVE IS THE CHEESE IN THE CASSEROLE OF LIFE!
OH BARF. THAT'S THE CHEESIEST THING I'VE EVER HEARD!
THANKS FOR RESCUING ME, SON. FEELS GOOD TO BE BRINGING HOME THE BACON.
NO PROBLEMA, POP.
ALL THIS WRINKLING MAKES ME HUNGRY FOR BROCCOLI. WEIRD.

NO GUTS, NO GLORY

After school today, Bee and Danny and I walked in the rain to Goosy's house. She took us to her art studio and handed us each a smock, a pair of safety goggles, and a black marker. She'd covered a long table with plastic, and on top of the plastic sat 5 enormous pumpkins.

"Oh my gosh!" said Bee. "They're too beautiful to carve!"

"Wow!" signed Danny. (To say "wow" in sign language, you just spread the fingers on your right hand, with your palm facing toward your body, then raise your hand to about shoulder-level and shake it up and down 2 times. I may be terrible at Spanish, but I'm getting pretty good at deaf language.)

PRETEND YOU'RE TRYING TO FLING SOMETHING GROSS OFF YOUR FINGERS.

"Let's get carvin'!" I said. "Chop-chop. We've got business to attend to after this pumpkin thing."

"Homework?" asked Goosy.

"Tomorrow's Halloween!" I said. "We can't study at a time like this! Tonight we must devote every ounce of energy to devising the perfect trick-or-treating plan. Our success depends on it."

"Sounds serious," said Goosy.

"Aldo wants to collect tons of Halloween candy this year," explained Bee. "He wants to get more than Jack does."

"Where is the Jackster, anyway?" asked Goosy as she picked up a marker and drew a pattern on the front of her pumpkin. "I picked out that skinny pumpkin just for him."

"Jack is mad," signed Danny with goopy hands. He'd already cut the lid off his pumpkin and was scooping out the slimy, wet guts.

"Mad about what?" asked Goosy.

"He's exasperated* that Aldo doesn't appreciate the Spanish language," shrugged Bee.

"I do so!" I protested. "For example, enchiladas and empanadas are pretty much my favorite foods! And taquitos! Let's not forget about taquitos!"

"Hm. I don't think that counts," Goosy said. "What do you think, Danny?" As she spoke, she also sign languaged to him. (Goosy's been taking sign language classes at old-people school.) And when Danny stopped pumpkin-gutting to answer her question, she translated for him:

"When people can't communicate with me, it's frustrating. For both of us," he said. "But when people don't even <u>try</u> to speak my language...it's like they've decided my language isn't good enough. That <u>I'm</u> not good enough."

My eyes watched Danny say what he had to say as my ears listened to Goosy interpret for him. And inside me, in my guts, my electron of sadness must have had a eureka moment, too, because I could feel it wake up and start whizzing around again.

That's when I felt something small and wet splat against my cheek. "Ew! What was that?!" I yelped. Then I felt another. Then 2 more. It was Goosy! She was flinging goopified pumpkin seeds at me!

"Pumpkin guts fight!" hollered Goosy, and she chucked a whole handful of muck in my direction. By now Bee and Danny had joined in, and pumpkin intestines were flying every which way. It was the gloppiest mess I'd ever helped make, but it was also the funniest. If you ever need a good laugh, toss a bunch of pumpkin guts at your grandma's head. But only if she's a good sport, like mine is.

When the mush finally settled, Goosy sent us out into the rain to rinse off while she cleaned up the studio a little. Then we went back inside and finished carving our Halloween pumpkins.

"We still need a trick-or-treating plan," I said to Bee and Danny as I cut out my elaborate* design, "one that will maximize candy and minimize walking. I say we start at my house then head this way. Goosy, whaddya giving out this year?"

"Everlasting Gobstoppers," said Goosy. "Best candy of all time."

"Not bad...," I said. "Can we just get some tonight? Save us a walk? C'mon...Halloween is tomorrow..."

"No way José," she said.

"I checked on Weather Underground," said Bee, "and it's supposed to rain really hard tomorrow night."

"Dang! How are we gonna keep our candy dry?" I worried.

Danny grabbed a big plastic bag that was sitting on Goosy's work table and tugged it over the top of his pumpkin.

"Good idea! We'll make little rain ponchos for our pillowcases."

Before we left, Goosy set the timer on her camera and took a picture of all of us:

Funny how they're called jack-o'-lanterns and Jack wasn't even there.

HALLOWEEN NIGHT

IT'S A SCARY, CLIMACTIC CHAPTER. DON'T SAY I DIDN'T WARN YOU!

So much happened tonight that I don't know if I can cram it all into the few blank pages left in my E sketchbook...but here goes.

First, Bee and Danny came to my house for dinner. On Halloween night, Dad always makes mummy dogs, which are hot dogs rolled up and baked in crescent roll strips then dotted with mustard to make the eyes and mouth. The perfect fuel to top off your trick-or-treating tank.

Then we put on our costumes and counted down the minutes till sunset, which (I looked it up) was 5:57 p.m. Everybody knows that for the best candy yield, you've gotta get going door-to-door the second the sun drops below the horizon.

While we were waiting, Mom got out the
walkie-talkies. They're these old-school radio dealies
that 2 people can use to talk to each other if
they're less than about a mile apart. Tonight was
the first Halloween I was allowed to go trick-or-
treating without Mom or Dad or Timothy, so the
walkie-talkies were to make my mom feel better.
Oh, and she made me take a stupid flashlight too.

Why didn't I just use my cell phone, you ask? Because I don't HAVE a cell phone! My parents won't let me get one till I'm in high school.

At 5:57 sharp, I clipped my walkie-talkie to my belt, grabbed my empty pillowcase in one hand and my umbrella in the other, and barked to Bee and Danny, "Let's go, people." And with that, the 3 of us headed out into the pouring rain.

First house: fun-size Snickers. Not so fun. Second house: Smarties. I don't think so. Third house: toothbrushes. You've got to be kidding me. At one point I saw a soggy Legolas (Jack) and a waterlogged Ewok (Tommy Geller) out of the corner of my face. They were crossing the street ahead of us. But I was bound and determined not to be distracted from my mission, so I soldiered on.

We'd scored only 1 full-size candy bar by the time we made it to Goosy's. She invited us in to dry off and rest for a minute (and take a handful each of Everlasting Gobstoppers). As I lay there like a saturated sponge, I peered into my pillowcase: still mighty empty.

DANG. THAT WAS SURE A LARGE AMOUNT OF PHYSICAL ACTIVITY FOR SUCH A SMALL AMOUNT OF CANDY.

"Enough dawdling!" I said to the troops. "It's 7:13 already. Let's move 'em out."

"But it's raining so much!" said Bee. "The streets are filling up with giant puddles!"

"Dangerous," Danny signed.

"Welp, the world is a dangerous place," I said. "But neither puddles nor rain nor thunder and lightning shall keep us from our appointed rounds! Onward!"

"¡Buena suerte!" honked Goosy as we left her house. "Be sure to use your walkie-talkie to call your parents if you need a ride!"

Bee was right about the puddles. The gutters ran curb-deep in rainwater, and the intersections looked more like lakes than streets. Plus, the sidewalks were deserted. We seemed to be the only kids still out in the storm.

But we kept going: Ding-dong, trick-or-treat!, bunch of candy—house after house after house. Now at every front door, our neighbors heaved great gobs of candy into our pillowcases because they knew we were the last trick-or-treaters of the night. Our pillowcases filled fast. I guess it's true... Every cloud does have a silver lining.*

We followed the street as it curved around and back toward Jack's house. I was just thinking, *Should we trick-or-treat at Jack's house? Awkward!* when magically, there was Jack, standing on the sidewalk in front of us. The rain was running down his Legolas cheeks like elf tears.

"Aldo, Abuelo is missing!"

"Whaddya mean he's missing?"

"My mom just realized he's not in the house. His coat is gone, too, so we think he came outside. But it's dark—and the streets are starting to flood. Help me find him!"

Poor Abuelo! And poor Jack! And just like that, I could feel my electron of sadness reattach itself—click!—to my Jack atom, which is where it belonged this whole time. It wasn't actually a sadness electron, after all—it was just a lost piece of a best friend atom.

"We'll help you," I said. "Don't worry. Everything will be fine."

"Let's split up so we can cover more ground," suggested Bee. "Danny and I will take the street where I live, and you each take yours. We'll meet at Jack's in half an hour to see if Abuelo's been found."

So I flicked on my flashlight and took off in the direction of my house. I waded through a giant puddle, which was ankle-deep. In the gutter, the rainwater was rushing faster and faster, like a mountain stream in springtime.

I'M ALWAYS RUNNING IN THIS BOOK!

Then, ahead of
me, I saw a
lone figure
in the middle
of the road. Lightning
flickered, and for an
instant I could see him
more clearly: the ghoul
with the black umbrella! He
was blocking my way! No,
he was coming toward me!

I stopped in my tracks and
put a hand on my walkie-
talkie. AAAH! I should call
Mom and Dad and run back
to Goosy's! I screamed inside. But then I remembered
my mission: my best friend was counting on me to
help save his grandfather. Would I be courageous
enough to risk my life in order to save someone? I
asked myself for the second time in 2 weeks—only
tonight, the question was for reals. The answer
rose within me like a belch of courage: Yyyes!

I tried to swing wide and run past the ghoul, but my heavy pillowcase was slowing me down. He angled toward me. Just as I was about to eke* by him, he reached out and grabbed me! His hand felt like a skeleton, strong and bony on my wrist.

I think I fainted for a second, then his voice woke me up. "¡Profesor!" he said clearly.

Profesor? I tried to shake his hand from my arm, but his grip was tight. I was going to die, right here and now, a block from my house, at the tender age of 10. I tried to scream but nothing came out. Then the ghoul said, "¡Profesor! ¡Ayúdame! Estoy perdido."

I recognized that voice! I pointed the flashlight at his face and saw it wasn't a ghoul, it wasn't Mr. Mot, it wasn't Señor Espinoza—it was Abuelo! He was scared because he was *perdido*—a word I remembered from Spanish class. He was lost. And he thought I was *Profesor*—Professor Albert Einstein! (My Einstein costume <u>was</u> pretty convincing, I have to admit.)

I patted him on the shoulder and took his arm. "*Hola*, Abeulo," I said. "Don't worry. I'm your *amigo*. I'll take you to Jack's *casa*."

But the water in the streets was now up to our knees and flowing fast. Just holding Abuelo by the arm wouldn't be enough. He was going to be swept away! So I heroically dropped my sack of candy into the current, hoisted Abuelo over my shoulder, and carried him to the side of the road.

IT'S A DILEMMA: HIS RAISINY HEAD OR MY RAISINETS?

WHY WAS I BORN WITH ONLY 2 HANDS?! WHYYY?!

Whew. We were both soaking wet, though, and Abuelo's teeth were chattering. I needed to get him inside. It was way too dangerous to walk him home, and I couldn't leave him alone. What was I going to do?

Lightbulb! We were standing at the edge of the park, right next to our fort tree. And what's the one place OUTSIDE that stays dry, even during bad weather? Yup!

So I helped Abuelo crawl under the branches into the fort. I took off my Einstein jacket and wrapped it around his shoulders. I was just about to turn on the walkie-talkie to call Mom and Dad when—*oh no!*—those round, yellow eyes appeared at the edge of the fort. And of course, they were headed toward us.

"AAAAAAH!" I screamed, out loud this time.

"*Mapache*," Abuelo said calmly. "Raccoon."

And sure enough, the glow-in-the-dark moon eyes belonged to a raccoon! Carrying a chunk of egg carton in his mouth, he lumbered right past us and climbed up the trunk of the fort tree into the darkness above.

"*Mapache*," I said. "¡*Mapache gordo!*" And I tapped the side of my nose two times. That made Abuelo laugh.

I called Mom and Dad. They came to rescue us in the pick-up truck, and together we brought Abuelo home to his *familia*.

Back at Jack's, Mrs. Lopez helped Abuelo change into dry clothes and a robe, then she wrapped him in a warm blanket. Afterwards, she made Mexican hot chocolate for everyone, and we sat around Jack's kitchen table and talked.

She said Abuelo has been sleeping during the day a lot and taking walks at weird hours. He doesn't tell her when he leaves the house, either—he just leaves, and then has trouble finding his way back.

"His memory's fading," she said as she kissed him on the top of his raisiny noggin. "I think that's why he's lost his English. And he's taken to wearing my pink scarf... haven't you, Papá?"

Abuelo just kept smiling his enigmatic* smile and sipping his hot chocolate.

Then I told my story of seeing the ghoul with the umbrella and later the yellow eyes that turned out to be a *mapache*. ("That means raccoon," I whispered to my mom and dad.) I told how I almost ran from the ghoul tonight but didn't. I told how I sacrificed my candy and carried Abuelo to safety.

"Thank you, Aldo," said Jack when it was time for me to go home. "I want you to have this." And he handed me his wet pillowcase filled halfway with candy.

"*De nada*, Joaquín," I said. But I took the candy anyway. I'm not <u>that</u> selfless!

HALF A PILLOWCASEFUL <u>IS</u> AN EPIC WIN AT THIS POINT.

HERE COMES THE SOL

I woke up this morning to sunshine pouring through my window. My eyeballs had gotten so used to dark and stormy during the last few weeks that it practically blinded me, but in a nice-surprise kind of way.

It was Friday morning, and even though I was super tired from all the excitement last night, it was a school day, so after a big breakfast of scrambled eggs and Halloween candy, I walked to Jack's and got a big hug from Mrs. Lopez. Then Jack and I ambled the rest of the way to school together, just like best friends do.

After school, Bee, Jack, Danny, Tommy, and I met in the fort for the annual Halloween candy exchange. We brought our pillowcases and dumped our candy into piles so it could be sorted, counted, and traded. Since Jack's candy was now my candy, we all shared with Jack. But the only kind he really likes is peanut butter cups, so that was easy.

"So Abuelo isn't actually doing top-secret science anymore, huh," I said to Jack as I counted out 111 Tootsie Rolls. "I thought he was, since he hides in closets and writes on notepads."

"Nope," said Jack. "He gets mixed up and goes into the closet sometimes because he thinks it's the door to his bedroom. And he writes things down so he won't forget them...but then he forgets that he wrote them down."

"It must be weird to start forgetting things," said Tommy.

"I can relate," I said. "I forget almost everything from Spanish class."

"I guess you're no Einstein after all," signed Danny, which made everyone chuckle.

Besides giving away almost all her candy, Bee brought beaded friendship bracelets for each of us that she made at EcoWeek.

"Wow, thanks Bee!" I said, and I stuffed mine deep into my coat pocket, which is where it will stay, unless it accidentally on purpose falls out someday very soon.

And even though I know you're not supposed to feed wildlife, I left a couple Tootsie Rolls in the knot of the tree for our messy friend the mapache.

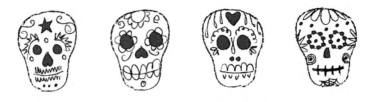

DÍA DE LOS MUERTOS

Today, November 2nd, is a holiday called the Day of the Dead, or *Día de los Muertos*. Jack's family was going to a party at the Erie Rec Center, and they invited my family to join them.

The rec center gym looked like somebody put a rainbow Slushie in a blender and forgot to put the lid on. You've never <u>seen</u> such crazy-bright decorations and costumes! Mixed in among all the colorful streamers and balloons and table coverings were photos of dead people. I mean, they didn't <u>look</u> dead in the pictures...they were smiling and happy and everything...but they were friends and family who used to be alive but aren't anymore.

Fortunately, Mexican people like to make amazing food to share with their dead loved ones too. The food at this Muertos celebration was so exquisitely delicious, <u>I</u> almost died—of pleasure!

There were also Mexican dancers in old-timey costumes and a mariachi band. My dad and Mr. Mot even went on stage and played a song on their guitars while Señor Espinoza sang the words in Spanish: "Bésame mucho..." (I'm pretty sure it was about kissing. Blech.)

Dancing is one of those activities that requires moving and balancing at the same time, so I sat with Abuelo while everyone else boogied. I nibbled on an empanada filled with appley-cinnamonness and tapped my toe to the beat. On the dance floor, Goosy twirled Jack around, and when he finished spinning, he laughed and waved at me.

"Mi amigo," Abuelo said to me. "¿Me traes una empanada?"

"Sure thing," I said. And I didn't just bring him one empanada. I brought him a whole plateful of different flavors so he wouldn't tenga hambre.

"E" GALLERY

Mr. Mot used to be an English teacher. He's a word nerd, and he likes to help me use awesome words in my sketchbooks. I mark the best words with one of these: * (it's called an asterisk). When you see an * you'll know you can look here, in the Gallery, to see what the word means. If you don't know how to say some of the words, just ask Mr. Mot. Or someone you know who's like Mr. Mot. Or go to aldozelnick.com, and we'll say them for you.

eager (pg. 98): ready and excited for something to happen

eccentric (pg. 20): different than other people in a noticeable kind of way

earsplitting (pg. 7): mega-loud; so loud your eardrums feel like they might split in 2

easy on the eyes (pg. 45): handsome

GO AHEAD. YOU DECIDE WHOSE PICTURE DESERVES TO BE NEXT TO "EASY ON THE EYES" IN THE GALLERY.

éclairs (pg. 10): these really yummy pastries with cream filling and chocolate on top

ecstasy (pg. 13): happiness squared

edible (pg. 19): eatable. So why don't we just say eatable?

edition, first (pg. 41): A first edition means a copy of the book from the first batch that was ever printed at the book factory.

eerie (pg. 8): creepy in a what-a-weird-coincidence kind of way

egads (pg. 32): an exclamation of surprise, like Oh my gosh! or Holy smokes!

egged on (pg. 91): encouraged (but more fun to say)

egghead (pg. 32): somebody who's so smart he's nerd-smart

eggplant (pg. 63): a giant jelly-bean-shaped veggie with purple skin

ego (pg. 72): pride in your own awesomeness

eke (pg. 129): just barely make it (different from "eek," which is the noise some people (not me) make when they see a mouse)

elaborate (pg. 119): fancy and detailed.

elated (pg. 49): really happy; close to ecstasy-level happiness

elbowing (pg. 27): pushing with your elbow

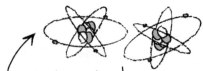

electrons (pg. 23): the can't-sit-still particles that fly in circles around the edge of an atom

enamored of (pg. 31): in love with

en garde (pg. 84): French for "on guard." You say it when you're sword-fighting for some reason.

endangered (pg. 95): in danger of being ruined

enigmatic (pg. 133): mysterious; seems unexplainable

enormous (pg. 94): really huge

enough is enough (pg. 93): Stop already, wouldja? I'm exasperated.

enthusiast (pg. 78): fan; aficionado

enticing (pg. 86): interesting; luring you in, like the popcorn smell in a movie theater. Or like bacon

entranced (pg. 61): attention grabbed and held by something; something that <u>entices</u> you pulls you in, but something that <u>entrances</u> you keeps your attention

epaulets (pg. 21): those fancy shoulder pads that army generals and Captain Crunch wear

epic (pg. 49): important in the whole history of the world

epicurean (pg. 13): having to do with fancy food

equations (pg. 40): math-ematical formulas with an equal sign, like $e=mc^2$

equivalent (pg. 57): 2 things that are basically the same

erudite (pg. 4, 41): well-educated and smart

escarole (pg. 122): fancy lettuce

Eskimo Pies (pg. 94): a kind of chocolate-covered ice cream on a stick

Español (pg. 4, 66): Spanish the way you say it in Spanish

essentials (pg. 78): the things you absolutely can't live without. Like bacon.

esteemed (pg. 41): respected

euphemism (pg. 86): a nicer way of saying something not so nice

eureka! (pg. 83): I've got it!

evaporate (pg. 21): disappear into a form you can't see

POOF!

everlastingly (pg. 3): forever and ever for always

Every cloud has a silver lining (pg. 125): This is a saying that means everything that's bad has a little good in it too.

exaggerating (pg. 86): making the truth sound more impressive than it really is

exasperated (pg. 117): fed up with

exceed (pg. 3): go beyond

exceptionally (pg. 6): especially so

exchange (pg. 29): trade; swap

exclaimed (pg. 32): said with lots of emotion! and exclamation points!!!

excruciatingly (pg. 55): uber painfully

exhausted (pg. 12): completely and totally pooped out

expectations (pg. 3): what someone already knows you can do

exquisite (pg. 53): one of the very best or most perfect of its kind. For example, I know this really exquisite 10-year-old boy named Aldo Zelnick...

extended (pg. 8): reached out; made longer

extraterrestrials (pg. 41): aliens; ET-types

eyeballing (pg. 50): looking at with, well, your eyeballs

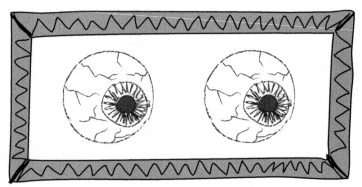

GALERÍA DE ESPAÑOL

abuelo (pg. 12 and lots of pages): grandfather

bienvenidos (pg. 35): welcome

buena suerte (pg. 125): good luck

bueno (pg. 75): good

casa (pg. 130): house

adiós, muchacho (pg. 69): goodbye, boy

almuerzo (pg. 33): lunch

amigo (pg. 38): friend

ayúdame (pg. 129): help me

¡Basta! (pg. 93): Enough!

bésame mucho (pg. 139): kiss me a lot (gross)

cuate (pg. 109): buddy; bro

cuchara (pg. 56): spoon

de nada (pg. 134): you're welcome

Día de los Muertos (pg. 138): Day of the Dead celebration

Donde está el cuarto de baño? (pg. 101): Where is the bathroom?

elefante estúpido (pg. 54): stupid elephant

empanadas (pg. 13): little pies with crust on all sides that you can eat with your hands

en (pg. 34): in

en Español, por favor (back cover): in Spanish, please

es mejor (pg. 35): It's better.

Este es mi amigo (pg. 38): This is my friend.

Estoy perdido (pg. 102): I'm lost.

excelente (pg. 55): excellent

familia (pg. 132): family

gordo (pg. 33): fat

hola (pg. 130): hello

luchador (pg. 18): a pro wrestler in Mexico

La práctica hace al maestro (pg. 67): practice makes perfect

mapache (pg. 132): raccoon

Me llamo Tocino (pg. 34): My name is Bacon.

me traes una empanada (pg. 139): bring me an empanada

mi barrio (pg. 152): my neighborhood

mi mejor amigo (pg. 4): my best friend

muy importante (back cover): very important

No entiendo (pg. 101): I don't understand.

No hablo Español (pg. 34): I don't speak Spanish.

No problema (pg. 114): No problem

No tengo un paraguas (pg. 34): I don't have an umbrella.

profesor (pg. 129): professor

¿Qué? (pg. 34): What?

Qué chido (pg. 53): Cool

¿Qué onda? (pg. 12): What's up?

¿Quién fue...? (pg. 29): Who was...

siempre llueve sobre mojado (pg. 3): when it rains it pours

señor (pg. 3): mister

sol (pg. 135): sun

¡Te amo! (pg. 33): I love you!

tengo hambre (pg. 100): I'm hungry.

tenga hambre (pg. 139): be hungry

vaso (pg. 57): glass

Venga (pg. 50): Come!

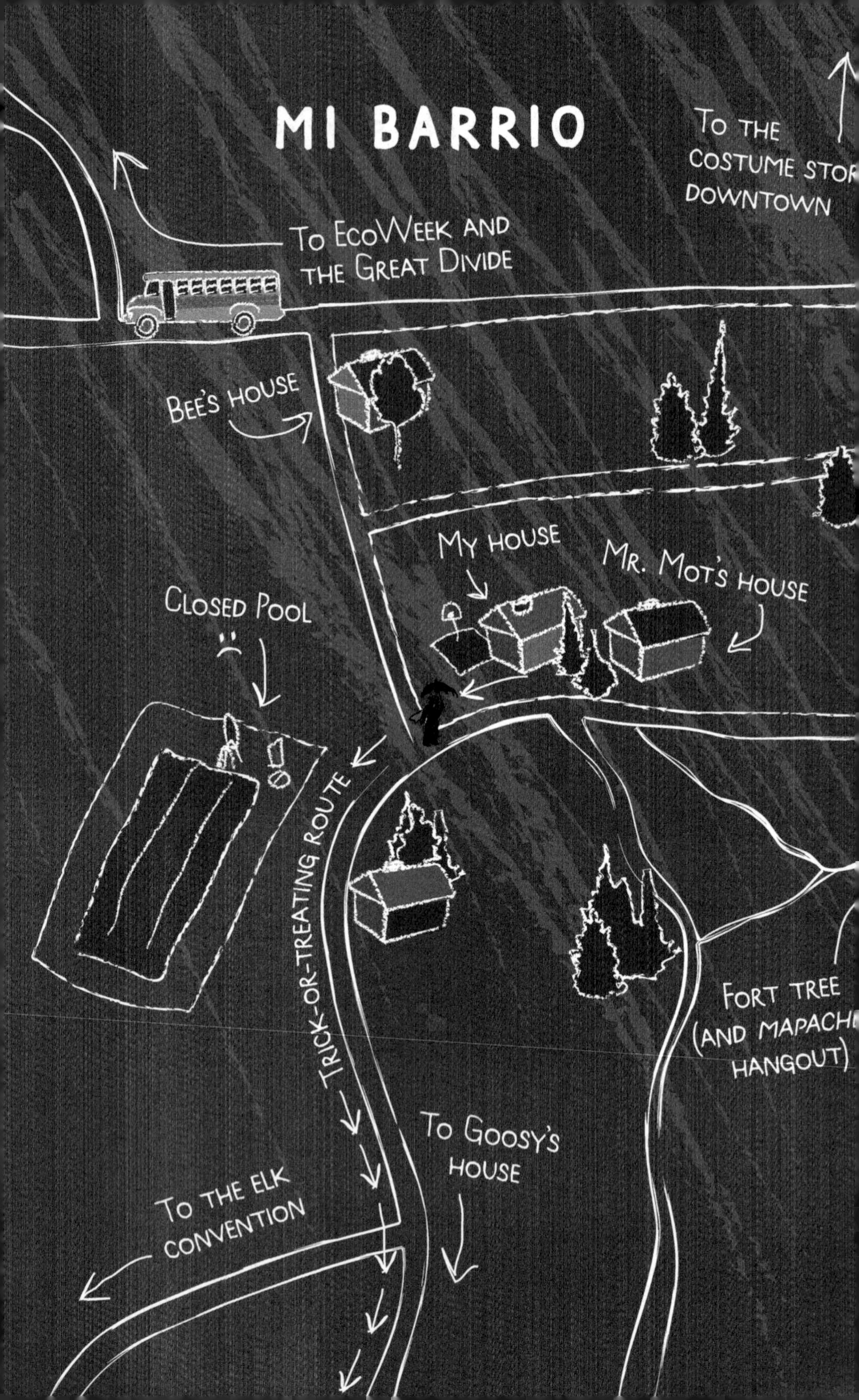
MI BARRIO
To the costume store downtown
To EcoWeek and the Great Divide
Bee's house
My house
Mr. Mot's house
Closed Pool
Trick-or-treating route
Fort tree (and mapache hangout)
To Goosy's house
To the Elk convention

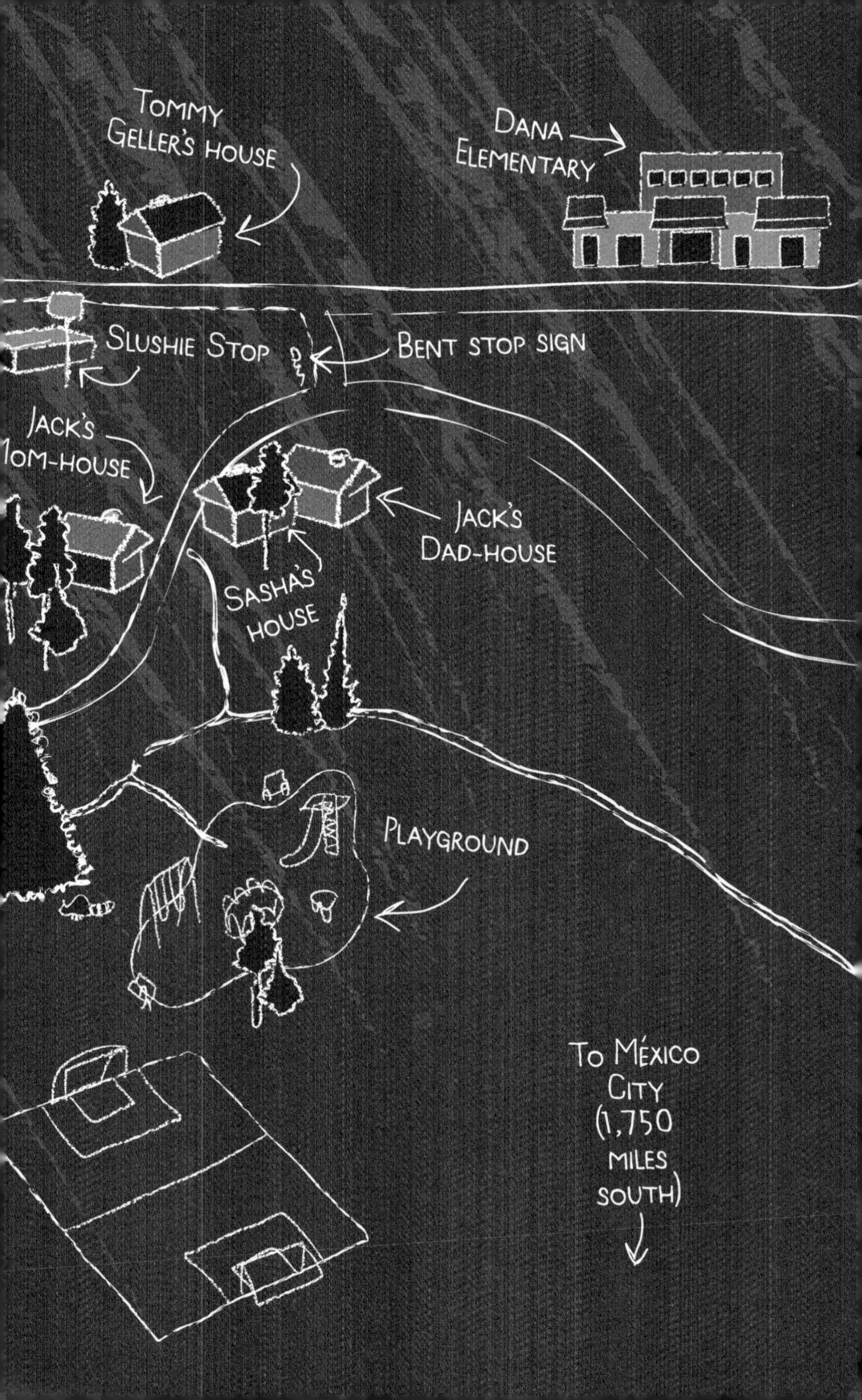
Tommy Geller's house
Dana Elementary
Slushie Stop
Bent stop sign
Jack's Mom-house
Jack's Dad-house
Sasha's house
Playground
To México City (1,750 miles south)

Sneak a Peek!

Dive right into the next book in the audacious Aldo Zelnick Series here.

FINICKY
EGGHEAD
DUMBSTRUCK
CAHOOTS
BOGUS!
ARTSY-FARTSY

AN EXCERPT FROM **FINICKY**, BOOK 6 IN THE ALDO ZELNICK SERIES!

PIZZA FAMINE?*

I DON'T LIKE THE SOUND OF "PIZZA FAMINE" ONE BIT.

YEAH. I HAVE A BAD FEELING IN MY BONES.

Ahhh. There's nothing like a slice of sausage pizza to put a big greasy smile on your face and a warm lump of bliss in your belly.

Today's Monday, so it was pizza lunch at Dana Elementary. The cafeteria serves pizza <u>every</u> Monday, which means on Sunday nights you have something to look forward to even though your weekend is, sadly, ancient history.

AN EXCERPT FROM **FINICKY**, BOOK 6 IN THE ALDO ZELNICK SERIES!

Even Jack likes pizza! I mean, there aren't many foods in this universe that my best friend will eat, but cheese pizza is one of them. He's so finicky* that he pretty much lives on peanut-butter sandwiches, plain bagels, noodles with butter, and cheese pizza. Our friend Bee says he's a beige-atarian.

So Jack and I were sitting there in the cafeteria enjoying Monday pizza. Bee was eating a salad she'd brought from home—green and red and orange and yellow all mixed together in a plastic bowl. It looked more like a Crayola shrub than a food, if you ask me.

AN EXCERPT FROM **FINICKY**, BOOK 6 IN THE ALDO ZELNICK SERIES!

That's when Mr. Fodder—he's a lunch lady who's a guy—walked up to us with a funny look on his face. He glanced both ways then leaned in close to whisper to me. His hairnetted beard was practically touching my cheek.

SAVOR THAT SAUSAGE PIZZA, ZELNICK. IT MIGHT BE YOUR LAST.

"Whaaa?" I choked. I can never tell whether Mr. Fodder is kidding or serious, but he had me seriously worried. "We have pizza <u>every</u> Monday!"

AN EXCERPT FROM *FINICKY*, BOOK 6 IN THE ALDO ZELNICK SERIES!

"There's talk of a new school menu," he shrugged. "Food that's 'healthier.'" He air-quoted around the word "healthier."

WHEN YOU "DRAW" QUOTATION MARKS IN THE AIR WITH YOUR FINGERS, IT MEANS YOU DON'T AGREE WITH THE WORDS YOU'RE PUTTING THE QUOTES AROUND. WEIRD.
(ALSO, JUST SO YOU KNOW, MR. FODDER THE LUNCH MAN IS NOT AS CRAZY OR AS CREEPY AS HE LOOKS.)

"But cheese pizza is one of my 4 food groups," mumbled Jack.

"Sorry kid," said Mr. Fodder. "Hate to be the bearer of nauseating news." And he and his beard wobbled away.

Jack and I turned to glare at Bee and her veggie-lovers' salad.

"What?" she said. "I didn't have anything to do with this! Although I just <u>know</u> you will adore vegetables once you get used to them. Oh! I hope they put fennel on the menu! Fennel rocks."

ARE YOU KIDDING ME?

PLEASE SAY YOU'RE KIDDING.

You ARE KIDDING, RIGHT?

HEY! I MAY NOT BE CORN, BUT I STILL HAVE EARS. AND FEELINGS!

I looked down at my last bite of pizza. I'd saved one flawless* pearl of sausage atop one perfect pillow of tomato-sauce-dotted crust. It glistened in the fluorescent* light shining down from the cafeteria ceiling. I placed it on closed my eyes, and chewed.

Somehow it wasn't as which is what can h favorite thin examinin

ACK!
WHAT HAPPENS NEXT?
Get your hands on the full book at aldozelnick.com or your local bookstore or library.

award-winning
ABOUT THE ~~ALDO ZELNICK~~
COMIC NOVEL SERIES

ABOUT THE **ALDO ZELNICK**
COMIC NOVEL SERIES

The Aldo Zelnick comic novels are an alphabetical series for middle-grade readers aged 7-13. Rabid and reluctant readers alike enjoy the intelligent humor and drawings as well as the action-packed stories. They've been called vitamin-fortified *Wimpy Kids*.

Part comic romps, part mysteries, and part sesquipedalian-fests (ask Mr. Mot), they're beloved by parents, teachers, and librarians as much as kids.

Artsy-Fartsy introduces ten-year-old Aldo, the star and narrator of the entire series, who lives with his family in Colorado. He's not athletic like his older brother, he's not a rock hound like his best friend, but he does like bacon. And when his artist grandmother, Goosy, gives him a sketchbook to "record all his artsy-fartsy ideas" during summer vacation, it turns out Aldo is a pretty good cartoonist.

In addition to an engaging cartoon story, each book in the series includes an illustrated glossary of fun and challenging words used throughout the book, such as *absurd*, *abominable*, and *audacious* in *Artsy-Fartsy* and *brazen*, *behemoth*, and *boisterous* in *Bogus*.

BAILIWICK PRESS

www.bailiwickpress.com | www.aldozelnick.com

ALSO IN THE ALDO ZELNICK COMIC NOVEL SERIES

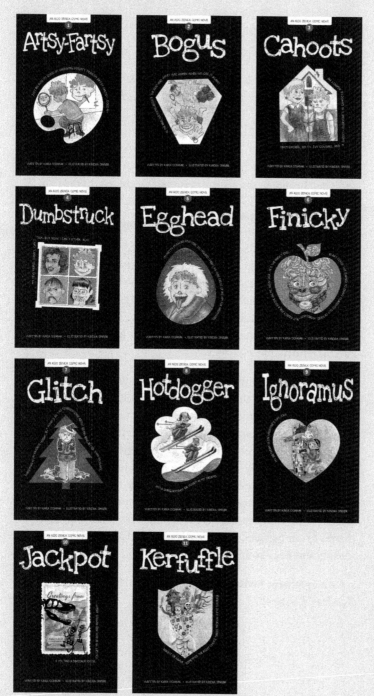

ACKNOWLEDGMENTS

"The pursuit of truth and beauty is a sphere of activity in which we are permitted to remain children all our lives."

— Albert Einstein

The Aldo Zelnick series is nothing if not our attempt to pursue truth and beauty in the most entertaining and, yes, childish manner imaginable.

Of all our books so far, *Egghead* especially exemplifies our childlike exuberance in eclecticism. Einstein, physics, *A Wrinkle in Time*, dark and stormy nights—they rub elbows well enough. (Plus, this year marks the 50th anniversary of Madeleine L'Engle's classic, so we couldn't resist.) But really...bilingualism, Halloween, Edward Gorey, and elder issues too? Thanks for humoring us. We'll always do our darnedest to repay the favor by humoring you, and your kids, in return.

We extend our gratitude to everyone who coddled *Egghead* into existence, including: the Little Shop of Physics at Colorado State University, whose director, Brian Jones, gave us permission to include the science experiments in this book; the Aldo enthusiasts at Independent Publishers Group; everything-doer Renée; excellent interns Brianna, Carolyn, Josh, and Justin; translator Sylvia Amorós, who eyeballed Aldo's Spanish; the Slow Sanders, for their endless encouragement and elucidation; and Launie, whose elegant design ensures Aldo is easy on the eyes. And as always, thanks to our families, who egg us on, and Aldo's Angels, who inexplicably keep coming back for more.

p.s. An epiphany! Elvis may have left the building, but you'll find Kendra on page 45.

ABOUT THE AUTHOR

Karla Oceanak has been a voracious reader her whole life and a writer and editor for more than twenty years. She has also ghostwritten numerous self-help books. Karla loves doing school visits and speaking to groups about children's literacy. She lives with her husband, Scott, their three boys, and a cat named Puck in a house strewn with Legos, ping-pong balls, Pokémon cards, video games, books, and dirty socks in Fort Collins, Colorado.

ABOUT THE ILLUSTRATOR

Kendra Spanjer divides her time between being "a writer who illustrates" and "an illustrator who writes." She decided to cultivate her artistic side after discovering that the best part of chemistry class was entertaining her peers (and her professor) with "The Daily Chem Book" comic. Since then, her diverse body of work has appeared in a number of group and solo art shows, book covers, marketing materials, fundraising events, and public places. When she invents spare time for herself to fill, Kendra enjoys skiing, cycling, exploring, discovering new music, watching trains go by, decorating cakes with her sister, making faces in the mirror, and playing with her dog, Puck.

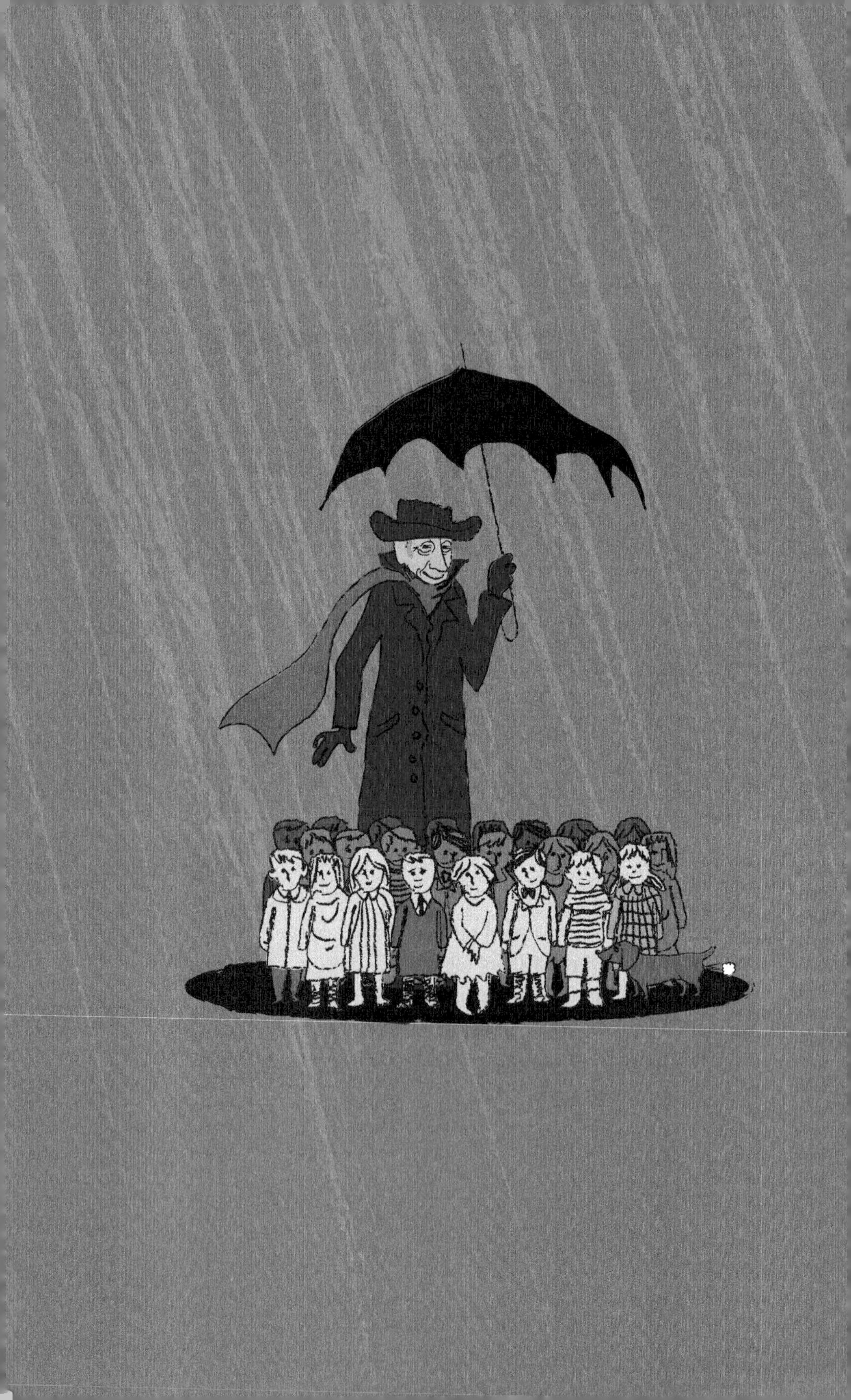